WILD BORN

The world is in peril.

A long-forgotten evil has risen from the far corners of Erdas, and we need YOU to help stop it.

Claim your spirit animal and join the adventure now:

1. Go to spiritanimals.com.

2. Log in to create your character and choose your own spirit animal.

3. Have your book ready and enter the code below to unlock the adventure.

Your code:

NRMR7XMFW2

By the Four Fallen,
   The Greencloaks

SPIRITANIMALS.COM

The ground began
to tremble. The sky
darkened. A brilliant
flash pierced the
gloom like lightning.

And then he saw
the wolf.

WILD BORN

Brandon Mull

SCHOLASTIC INC.

For Sadie, who loves animals.
And for Fluffy, Buffy, and Mango,
who are animals.
— B.M.

Library of Congress Control Number: 2013932302

ISBN 978-0-545-59971-9

10 9 8 7 6 5 4 3 2 1   13 14 15 16 17

Map illustration by Michael Walton
Book design by Charice Silverman

Library edition, September 2013

Printed in the U.S.A.   23

Scholastic US: 557 Broadway • New York, NY 10012
Scholastic Canada: 604 King Street West • Toronto, ON M5V 1E1
Scholastic New Zealand Limited: Private Bag 94407 • Greenmount, Manukau 2141
Scholastic UK Ltd.: Euston House • 24 Eversholt Street • London NW1 1DB

BRIGGAN

Given a choice, Conor would not have picked to spend the most important birthday of his life helping Devin Trunswick get dressed. In all honesty, he would not have volunteered to help Devin Trunswick do anything, ever.

But Devin was the eldest son of Eric, the Earl of Trunswick, and Conor was the third son of Fenray, Herder of Sheep. Fenray had incurred debts to the earl, and Conor was helping to work them off as a servant to Devin. The arrangement had begun over a year ago, and was set to last at least two more.

Conor had to hook each fiddly clasp on the back of Devin's coat correctly or the folds would hang crooked, and he would hear about it for weeks. The fine material was more decorative than practical. If caught in a storm, Conor knew that Devin would wish for a simpler, more durable coat. One without clasps. One that might actually keep him warm.

"Are you done fussing around back there?" Devin asked in exasperation.

"Sorry for the delay, milord," Conor replied. "There are forty-eight clasps. I'm just now linking the fortieth."

"How many more days will this take? I'm about to die of old age! Are you just inventing numbers?"

Conor resisted a sharp reply. Having grown up counting sheep, he probably knew his numbers better than Devin. But arguing with a noble caused more trouble than it was worth. Sometimes Devin seemed to deliberately tempt him. "It's my best guess."

The door flew open and Dawson, Devin's younger brother, burst into the room. "Are you *still* getting dressed, Devin?"

"Don't blame me," Devin protested. "Conor keeps napping."

Conor only gave Dawson a brief glance. The sooner he finished the clasps, the sooner he could get himself ready.

"How could Conor fall asleep?" Dawson called, giggling. "Everything you say, brother, is so *interesting*."

Conor resisted a grin. Dawson seldom stopped talking. He often got annoying, but he could sometimes be pretty funny. "I'm awake."

"Aren't you done yet?" Devin complained. "How many are left?"

Conor wanted to say twenty. "Five."

"Think you'll summon a spirit animal, Devin?" Dawson asked.

"I don't see why not," Devin replied. "Grandfather called a mongoose. Father produced a lynx."

Today was the Trunswick Nectar Ceremony. In less than an hour, the local children who turned eleven this month would each try to call a spirit animal. Conor knew that some families tended to form bestial bonds more regularly than others. Even so, calling a spirit animal was never guaranteed, no matter what your family name. There were only three kids scheduled to drink the Nectar, and the odds were against any of them succeeding. It was certainly nothing to boast about before it happened.

"What animal do you think you'll get?" Dawson wondered.

"Your guess is as good as mine," Devin said. "What do you expect?"

"A chipmunk," Dawson predicted.

Devin lunged at his brother, who scampered away, giggling. Dawson was not dressed as formally as his older brother, which allowed him freer movement. Still, Devin soon caught him and tackled him to the floor, pinning him down.

"A bear would be more likely," Devin said, grinding his elbow into his brother's chest. "Or a wildcat, like Father. First thing I'll do is have it taste you."

Conor tried to wait patiently. It wasn't his place to intervene.

"You might get nothing," Dawson said bravely.

"Then all I'll be is Earl of Trunswick, and your master."

"Not if Father outlives you."

"I'd mind my tongue, second son."

"I'm glad I'm not you!"

Devin twisted Dawson's nose until he yelped, then stood up, brushing off his trousers. "At least my nose isn't sore."

"Conor will drink the Nectar too!" Dawson cried. "Maybe he'll be the one to call a spirit animal."

Conor tried to look invisible. Did he hope to summon a spirit animal? Of course! Who wouldn't? You couldn't help hoping. Just because nobody in his family had done it since some obscure great-granduncle decades ago didn't make it impossible.

"Right." Devin chuckled. "And I suppose the smith's daughter will summon one as well."

"You never know," Dawson said, sitting up and rubbing his nose. "Conor, what would you like to have?"

Conor stared at the floor. He had been asked a direct question by a noble, so he had to answer. "I've always gotten on well with dogs. I'd like a sheepdog, I guess."

"What an imagination!" Devin laughed. "The sheepherder dreams of calling a sheepdog."

"A dog would be fun," Dawson said.

"And common," Devin said. "How many dogs do you have, Conor?"

"My family? Ten, last I counted."

"How long since you've seen your family?" Dawson asked.

Conor tried to keep his voice even. "More than half a year."

"They'll be there today?"

"I expect they'll try. It depends on whether they can get away." In case they couldn't make it, he didn't want to show that he cared.

"How novel for you," Devin sniffed. "How many clasps remain?"

"Three."

Devin turned around. "Let's not dawdle. We're running late."

◄━━●━━►

An impressive assemblage had gathered in the square. It was not every day that the son of a great lord quested for his spirit animal. Commoners and nobles alike had come for the event – old, young, and in between. Musicians played, soldiers strutted, and a peddler sold candied nuts. A grandstand had been erected for the earl and his family. Conor thought it looked as if a holiday had been declared. A holiday for everyone but him. The day was cool and clear. The green hills where Conor would rather be roaming loomed far beyond the blue rooftops and chimneys of Trunswick.

Conor had attended a few Nectar ceremonies. He had never witnessed the calling of a spirit animal, although he knew it had happened several times in this square during his lifetime. There had been little pageantry at the ceremonies he had seen. None had been well attended. And none had involved so many animals.

A common belief held that bringing together a variety of animals increased the chance of summoning a spirit animal. If so, Devin might be in luck. Not only were many domestic animals present, but Conor saw mews full of birds with exotic plumage, a corral containing deer and moose, several caged wildcats, a penned trio of badgers, and a black bear chained to a post by an iron collar. There was even a beast that Conor had only heard about in stories – a huge camel with two furry humps.

As Conor walked toward the center of the square, the

hordes of onlookers made him self-conscious. He wasn't sure what to do with his hands. Should he fold his arms or let them dangle at his sides? As he scanned the intimidating crowd, he tried to remember that most eyes were fixed on Devin.

Suddenly Conor noticed his mother waving. His elder brothers stood beside her, and his father. They had even brought Soldier, Conor's favorite sheepdog.

They had all made it! The sight of them thawed some of his fear and awoke a longing for home – meadows to wander, creeks to swim in, groves to explore. His work had been honest and outdoors – chopping wood, shearing sheep, feeding dogs. Their home had been small but cozy, and nothing like the drafty immensity of the earl's castle. Conor gave his mother a little wave.

The future Earl of Trunswick led the way to a bench near the center of the square. Abby, the smith's daughter, awaited them, sitting still and looking overwhelmed. She was clearly dressed in her best clothes, which were laughably inferior to even the most casual dress owned by Devin's mother or sister. Conor knew he must also look very plain beside Devin.

A pair of Greencloaks stood before the bench. Conor recognized the woman, Isilla, her graying hair gathered up in a glittering net over her pale face. Her goldfinch, Frida, was perched on her shoulder. Isilla normally officiated at the Nectar ceremonies. She had given the Nectar to both of his brothers.

The other Greencloak was a stranger, tall and lean, with wide shoulders and features as weathered as his cloak. His skin was darker than the people around him, as if he came from northeastern Nilo or southwestern Zhong – an unusual sight in the middle of Eura. His animal was not evident, but Conor noticed a hint of a tattoo winding away into his sleeve. The sight gave him a thrill. It meant the stranger's spirit animal was currently hibernating on his arm.

Abby rose and curtsied as Devin approached the bench. He sat down and motioned for Conor to follow his lead. Conor and Abby sat.

Isilla raised her hands to still the crowd. The stranger backed away, leaving her the center of attention. Conor wondered why the man had come. As with the rest of the pageantry, Conor decided it must be another nod to Devin's high status.

Isilla began in a penetrating voice, "Hear ye, hear ye, good people of Trunswick! Before the eyes of man and beast, we are gathered here today to participate in the most sacred rite in all of Erdas. When human and animal unite, their greatness is multiplied. We have come to witness whether the Nectar will reveal such greatness in any of these three candidates – Lord Devin Trunswick; Abby, daughter of Grall; and Conor, son of Fenray."

The cheering after the mention of Devin all but drowned out the other two names. Conor tried to remain impassive. If he sat still and kept calm, soon it would be over. Devin would drink the Nectar first, in the place of honor. Common belief held that the first to drink the Nectar in a ceremony was the most likely to call a spirit animal.

Isilla bent over to raise a plugged flask, the leather tooled with intricate designs. After raising the flask above her head to display it to the assemblage, she unstopped it. "Devin Trunswick, come forward."

The crowd whistled and clapped as Devin approached Isilla, then quieted down as she put her finger to her lips. Devin knelt before her, a sight Conor had seldom seen. Euran nobles only knelt to greater Euran nobles. The Greencloaks knelt to none.

"Receive the Nectar of Ninani."

Conor could not help but feel excited as the flask tipped toward Devin's lips. This might be the first time he witnessed a spirit animal summoned from the unknown! With all of these animals present, how could the Nectar fail? Conor wondered what the beast would look like.

Devin swallowed. Isilla stepped back. A deep hush fell over the square. Eyes closed, Devin tilted his face skyward. An empty moment passed. Somebody coughed. Nothing out of the ordinary was happening. Perplexed, Devin looked around.

Conor had heard that a spirit animal either came right after the Nectar was tasted, or never. Devin arose and turned in a full circle, eyes roving. There was no sign of anything appearing nearby. The crowd began to murmur.

Isilla hesitated, considering the grandstand. Conor followed her gaze. The earl sat grimly on his throne, his lynx nearby. Although he had summoned a spirit animal, he had chosen not to wear the green cloak.

Isilla glanced back at the foreign Greencloak, who gave a faint nod. "Thank you, Devin," she intoned. "Abby, daughter of Grall, come forward."

Devin looked queasy. His eyes were blank, but his

posture betrayed his humiliation. He glanced furtively toward his father, then looked down. When he lifted his eyes again, his gaze had hardened, the shame turning to fury. Conor looked away. It would be best to avoid Devin's attention for a while.

Abby drank and, as Conor expected, nothing happened. She returned to the bench.

"Conor, son of Fenray, come forward."

Hearing his name called gave Conor a nervous thrill. If Devin had failed to call an animal, Conor doubted he had any chance. Still, anything could happen. Never had so many eyes been trained just on him. Rising to his feet, Conor tried to ignore the crowd by focusing on Isilla. The tactic didn't really work.

If nothing else, it would be interesting to discover what the Nectar tasted like. His oldest brother had compared it to sour goat's milk, but Wallace liked to tease. His other brother, Garrin, had likened it to apple cider. Conor licked his lips. Whatever the taste, sampling the Nectar would officially mark the end of his childhood.

Conor knelt before Isilla. She looked down at him with a strange smile, curiosity lurking behind her eyes. Had she stared at the others this way?

"Receive the Nectar of Ninani."

Conor put his lips to the offered flask. The Nectar was thick, like syrup, and richly sweet, like fruit in honey. The consistency became more liquid once it was in his mouth. He swallowed. It tasted amazing! Better than anything he had ever tried.

Isilla withdrew the flask before he could steal another sip. One swallow was all he would ever sample. Conor stood in order to return to the bench and a burning, tingling sensation spread through his chest.

Animals began to cry out. The birds shrilled. The wildcats yowled. The bear roared. The moose trumpeted. The camel snorted and stomped.

The ground began to tremble. The sky darkened, as if a swift cloud had overtaken the sun. A brilliant flash pierced the gloom like lightning, but much nearer than any lightning Conor had experienced, nearer even than the time he saw a tree struck at the crest of a hill he was climbing.

Onlookers gasped and murmured. Dazzled by the flash, Conor blinked repeatedly to restore his vision. Hot tingles spread from his chest along his limbs. Despite the oddness of the moment, he felt irrationally joyful.

And then he saw the wolf.

Much like any sheepherder in the region, Conor had experience with wolves. Wolf packs had stolen many sheep under his care. Wolves had killed three of his favorite dogs over the years. Livestock lost to wolves was a big part of the reason his father had become indebted to the earl. And of course there was that night two years ago, when Conor and his brothers had stood against a brazen pack that had tried to steal sheep out of their pen in the high pasture.

Now the largest wolf he had ever seen stood before him, head held high. It was a remarkable creature – long-limbed, well fed, with the most luxurious coat of gray-white fur Conor could have imagined. He took in large paws, keen claws, savage teeth, and striking cobalt-blue eyes.

Blue eyes?

In the history of Erdas, only one wolf had such deep blue eyes.

Conor glanced at the Euran flag hanging from the earl's grandstand. Briggan the Wolf, patron beast of Eura, stood depicted upon a rich blue banner, eyes shrewd and piercing.

The wolf padded forward calmly, stopping directly before Conor. It sat, like a trained dog yielding to its master. Its head came well above Conor's waist. Muscles tense, Conor resisted the impulse to leap away. Under other circumstances, he would have run from this animal, or yelled at it. He would have thrown rocks or grabbed a stout staff to defend himself. But this was no chance encounter out in the wild. His whole body was tingling, almost vibrating, and hundreds of people were watching. This wolf had appeared out of nowhere!

The wolf stared up at him with confidence. Though large and fierce, the animal seemed very much in control of itself. Conor was awed that a predator such as this would show him so much respect. Those blue eyes hinted at a greater understanding than any animal should possess. The wolf was waiting for something.

Conor held out a trembling hand and the wolf's warm pink tongue caressed his palm. The touch was electric, and the tingling in Conor's chest immediately ceased.

For an instant, Conor felt courage, and clarity, and an alertness like he had never known. He smelled the wolf with enhanced senses, and somehow knew it was male, and that it considered him an equal.

Then the strange moment of expanded perception passed.

In spite of the abundant evidence, it was the look on Devin Trunswick's face that brought home to Conor what had transpired. Never had Conor been the focus of such naked rage and envy. He had summoned a spirit animal!

And not just any spirit animal. A wolf. Nobody summoned wolves! Briggan the Wolf had been one of the Great Beasts, and spirit animals were never the same species as the Great Beasts. Everyone knew that. It simply didn't happen.

Yet it had. Undeniably, inexplicably, it had. A full-grown wolf was nuzzling Conor's palm. A wolf with deep blue eyes.

The bewildered crowd kept silent. The earl leaned forward attentively. Devin seethed, and Dawson's mouth was spread in an astonished grin.

The stranger in the green cloak approached and took Conor's hand. "I am Tarik," the man said in a low voice. "I came a long way to find you. Stay near me, and I will let no harm befall you. I won't press you to take our vows until you're ready, but you need to hear me out. Much depends on you."

Conor nodded numbly. It was all too much to digest.

The foreign Greencloak raised Conor's hand high and spoke in a powerful voice. "Good people of Trunswick! News of this day will echo across all of Erdas! In our hour of need, Briggan has returned!"

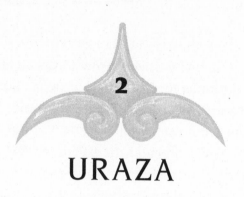

2

URAZA

Staying low, Abeke stalked through the tall grass, moving at a slow, steady pace. She stepped carefully, as her father had taught her, advancing in silence. Sudden motion or sounds would send her prey running. If this one got away, she wouldn't have time to approach another.

The antelope lowered its head to nibble at the grass. It was young, but she knew that it could easily outrun her. If it bounded away, she would return empty-handed.

Coming to a standstill, Abeke eased an arrow to the string of her bow. As she pulled it back, the bow creaked. The antelope abruptly looked up. The arrow flew true, skewering the beast's heart and lungs from the side. The antelope staggered only briefly before collapsing.

This antelope would matter to Abeke's village. The drought had made food scarce, and since it showed no sign of relenting, every morsel counted. Abeke knelt beside the fallen animal and spoke in a soft voice. "I'm sorry for taking your life, friend. Our village needs your meat. I got in close and made a clean shot so you wouldn't suffer. Please forgive me."

Abeke glanced at the bright sky. The sun had moved more than she had realized. How long had she stalked her prey? Fortunately, she had found game that was small enough to carry. Abeke slung the antelope over her shoulders and started home.

The sun glared down at the baked, brown plain. The brush was dry and brittle, the shrubs withered and thirsty. A few lonely baobab trees stood in the distance, trunks thick, branches sprawling, blurred by shimmering ripples of heat.

Abeke kept her eyes and ears open. People were not the prey of choice for big cats, but that became less certain when food grew scarce. And big cats were not the only dangerous animals roaming the Niloan savannah. Anyone who ventured beyond the village palisade took a risk.

The farther Abeke walked, the heavier the antelope seemed. But she was tall for her age, and had always been strong, and she was excited to show her prize to her father. She tried to ignore the hot sun.

In her village, the men normally did the hunting. Women rarely ventured out alone. What a surprise this antelope would be! What a perfect way to commemorate her eleventh nameday.

Her sister, Soama, might be more beautiful. She might sing and dance better. She might weave better. She might even be a more gifted artisan.

But she had never made a kill.

Just over a year ago, Soama had presented the village

with a beaded tapestry on her eleventh nameday, depicting herons in flight over a pond. Many had remarked that it was the most impressive work they had seen from a young artist. But could they eat it in a famine? Would the beaded pond cure their thirst? Would the fake herons ease the pains of their hunger?

Abeke could not resist a smile. To her knowledge, no child had ever brought game as a nameday gift. Did the village need another decorative jar? To hold what water? Her gift would serve a purpose.

To avoid being spotted by the lookouts, Abeke approached her village stealthily. She entered how she had exited—through the damaged slats in the side of the wall facing the ravine. There was some tricky climbing involved, made no easier by the carcass on her shoulders, but Abeke succeeded.

Time was short. Ignoring the stares of her neighbors, Abeke hurried to her home. Like most of the other dwellings in her village, her rondavel had a round base, with stone walls and a conical thatched roof. When she burst inside, she found Soama waiting, looking gorgeous in an orange wrap and a beaded scarf. Abeke was not bad-looking herself, but had long ago lost the contest of beauty to her sister. In any case, she favored more practical clothing, and braids that could be tied back.

"Abeke!" Soama said. "Where have you been? Does Father know you're back?"

"I went hunting," Abeke explained proudly, the antelope still resting on her shoulders. "Alone."

"You went outside? Past the gate?"

"Where else would I get an antelope?"

Soama put a brown hand over her eyes. "Abeke, why must you be so strange? You vanished. Father was worried! You're late for your bonding ritual."

"It'll be all right," Abeke assured her sister. "I'll hurry. I'm not as fussy as you. Nobody will complain once they see my fine kill."

Behind Abeke, the door opened. She turned and looked up at her father, a tall man, lean and muscular, with a shaved head. His eyes were not friendly. "Abeke! Chinwe told me you had returned. I was preparing a group to go search for you."

"I wanted to offer a fine nameday gift," Abeke explained. "I brought home this antelope."

Breathing heavily, her father closed his eyes. He could barely keep control of his tone. "Abeke. Today is important. You are late. You are covered in dust and blood. Your disappearance has put the village in an uproar. Have you no sense? Have you no dignity?"

Abeke withered inside, her pride dissolving, her happiness spoiling. For a moment she could find no reply. Tears threatened to fall. "But . . . I came to no harm. You know how well I hunt. This was a surprise."

Her father shook his head. "This was selfishness. Wrongheadedness. You cannot offer the antelope as your nameday gift! It is evidence of your misbehavior. What would it say about you? About us? What lesson will it teach other children? You will offer the jar you made."

"But the jar is ugly!" Abeke said desperately. "An ape could make a better one. I have no talent there."

"You make no effort there," her father said. "Returning alive with a kill shows skill, but it also shows poor judgment. We will discuss a punishment later. Make yourself ready. I will go tell the others that we will have your bonding ritual after all. Let Soama help you. If you would look to her example, you would disgrace us less."

Abeke felt desolate. "Yes, Father."

After her father left, Abeke unslung the antelope from her shoulders and set it down. Now that she was paying attention, she saw that her father was right—she was covered in dust and blood. She stared flatly at her fine kill. It had become a trophy of shame.

Abeke could barely restrain her tears. Today was supposed to be her day! Her one day. Everything was always about Soama. How thoughtful she was. How lovely. How talented. Today Abeke would drink the Nectar of Ninani. Would she call a spirit animal? Probably not. But today she became a woman. A true citizen of the village. And she had wanted to contribute a special gift.

Abeke wished for her mother. Her mother had understood her better than anyone. But her mother had never been strong, and had been taken by sickness.

Finally surrendering, Abeke started to weep.

"No time for that," Soama ordered. "You're late, and you look bad enough already."

Gritting her teeth, Abeke fought her emotions. Did she want her sister to see her cry? "What should I do?"

Soama crossed to her and wiped the tears from her cheeks. "On second thought, maybe you should cry. We don't have enough water to wash you."

"I'm done crying."

"Let's get you clean."

Abeke became as passive as a doll. She didn't complain

about the scratchy brushes or the barely damp cloth. She didn't offer any opinions about her outfit or her accessories. Abeke let Soama arrange everything, and tried not to look at her antelope.

When Abeke emerged, she found the whole village waiting. After all, today was her day. Starting at her door, everyone stood in two long lines forming a pathway. Abeke had looked forward to this. It had been fun to do it for others.

Her father stared at her sternly – as did most of the other men. Some of the women observed her with disgust, others with pity. A few of her younger acquaintances snickered.

Abeke walked between the people of her village, keenly aware of how she had disappointed them. She wished she could run away and get eaten by a lion.

Instead, she clutched the awful jug at her side, held her head high, and kept walking. The wind had risen, blowing dust. A cloud muted the sun. Abeke did not smile. She kept her expression neutral.

Abeke followed the winding path of people. After she passed, the lines behind her collapsed as everyone followed her to her destination.

Up ahead, Abeke spotted Chinwe. Standing beyond the end of the path, she wore the green cloak only brought out for bonding rituals, draped casually over one shoulder. The tattoo of her wildebeest was visible on her thin, bare leg.

As Abeke approached, Chinwe started chanting. The villagers echoed each phrase using the old tribal language. Abeke didn't know what most of the words meant, and neither did the others, but it was tradition.

When Abeke reached Chinwe, she knelt, feeling the gritty dirt beneath her bare knees. Still chanting, Chinwe dipped a small bowl into a large vessel and gazed down at Abeke. She didn't look angry or disapproving. She looked the same as she did during any bonding ritual – relaxed, and maybe a little bored.

Chinwe offered the bowl and Abeke accepted it. There was only a little fluid at the bottom, colorless like water, but thicker. She drank it. The Nectar tasted like unheated soup, the kind her mother used to make with crushed nuts. It was sweeter, but otherwise strikingly similar. The taste brought tears to Abeke's eyes.

Handing the bowl back, Abeke looked up at Chinwe curiously. Had that really been the Nectar? Or had Chinwe replaced the Nectar with root-and-nut soup? Chinwe took the bowl from Abeke and kept chanting.

Abeke felt unsteady, sort of dizzy and charged. Did everyone have this reaction? Her senses reached wide. She caught the vivid smell of rain on the wind. She could single out each individual chanting voice, and could tell who was off pitch. She could even hear her father and her sister.

The sky rumbled and darkened. The chanting broke off as everyone looked upward. Only once had Abeke seen a spirit animal called. Hano had done it, the grand-nephew of the old Rain Dancer. Abeke had been six at the time, but she didn't recall any thunder. A soft glow had appeared behind Hano, and an anteater had ambled out of the radiance.

There was nothing soft about this light. A dazzling column blazed into existence, more intense than a bonfire, casting long shadows around the village. Several people shrieked. When the light disappeared, a leopard remained. Buzzing from head to toe, Abeke stared in wonder. The leopard was large and sleek, almost the size of a lion. Her glossy hide was flawless. Out in the wild, standing this close to such a cat would have been the last thing Abeke ever did.

Nobody spoke. Muscles churning under her pelt, the great leopard walked to Abeke with liquid grace, and nuzzled her leg. Upon contact, the charge throughout Abeke's body vanished.

Acting on reflex, Abeke coiled slightly. The village suddenly seemed foreign and confining. She needed to get away! What if she jumped? She had the impression that if she desired, she could spring onto the nearest rooftop. She wanted to run free on the savannah, to prowl and hunt and climb.

The leopard rubbed against her hip and brought her back from the bewildering rush of instincts. Abeke straightened, hardly able to believe what was happening. The animal beside her could kill her with a single bite.

"It looks like Uraza," a child said, breaking the silence.

The comment started a wave of murmurs. The leopard prowled a few paces away from Abeke, almost as if uninterested, but then looked back. The cat did look like Uraza! She even had those legendary violet eyes, flashy as amethysts. But that was impossible. People didn't summon leopards. Cheetahs maybe, but never leopards or lions, let alone leopards with violet eyes.

Thunder grumbled overhead, and rain began to fall. What started gently soon became a downpour. People tilted their heads skyward, mouths open, arms extended. The crowd offered up laughter and joyful exclamations. A hand gripped Abeke's wrist. It was Chinwe. She wore a rare smile. "I believe we have found our new Rain Dancer."

The old Rain Dancer had died more than two years ago. Rain had not fallen on the village of Okaihee since. A few little storms had come close, but not a drop had landed within their walls. Several of the reliable wells had dried up. There had been much debate about how they would break the curse.

"A Rain Dancer?" Abeke marveled.

"It would be difficult to argue against it," Chinwe said.

Abeke's father approached, eyeing the leopard warily. "We should get indoors."

Abeke squinted at him through the downpour. "Can you believe this?"

"Truly, I cannot." He seemed distant. Was he still angry with her?

"Your daughter has ended our drought," Chinwe said.

"So it would appear."

"And she has summoned a leopard. Perhaps *the* leopard."

Her father nodded pensively. "The lost guardian of Nilo. What does this mean, Chinwe?"

"I don't know," Chinwe said. "It goes against . . . I'll have to consult someone who sees more deeply."

Her father considered the leopard. "Is it safe?"

Chinwe shrugged. "As safe as any wild thing can be. It's her spirit animal."

Her father regarded Abeke, droplets bombarding his bald head. "The rain is making up for lost time. Come."

Jogging after her father, her fancy wrap soaked, Abeke tried to understand why he seemed displeased. "Are you disappointed?" she ventured.

He stopped and gripped her shoulders, heedless of the rain. "I am confounded. I should be happy that you summoned an animal. But you have called a leopard! And not just any leopard – one that resembles our legendary guardian. In good ways and bad, you have always been different. And now this tops all of it! Will your beast bring good or evil upon you? Upon us? I don't know what to think."

The leopard gave a low growl, not terribly threatening, but not pleased either. Abeke's father turned and led the way to their home. The leopard followed behind. When they reached the front door, they found a stranger waiting. He wore Euran clothing – boots, trousers, and a lavish blue cloak with the hood raised against the rain. The hood obscured his face.

Abeke's father stopped near him. "Who are you?"

"I'm called Zerif," the man replied in a lively voice. "I journeyed here from afar. Your daughter has accomplished the impossible, as was foretold weeks ago by Yumaris the Inscrutable, one of the wisest women in all of Erdas. What happened today will reshape the world. I'm here to help."

"Then, enter," her father said. "I am Pojalo."

The three of them went through the doorway. The leopard followed smoothly.

Soama awaited them, her outfit damp but not soaked.

She must have hurried indoors. "There it is," she said, cautious eyes on the leopard. "Am I dreaming?"

"Isn't she amazing?" Abeke said, hoping her sister would be impressed. The leopard briefly sniffed the room, then crouched beside Abeke. Stooping, Abeke stroked the damp fur, not minding the smell of it.

"I don't feel safe," Soama said. She looked to her father for help. "Must it be indoors with us?"

"She belongs with me," Abeke replied immediately.

The stranger lowered his hood. He was middle-aged, with light brown skin and a neatly sculpted beard that only covered the end of his chin. "Perhaps I can help. This must all feel confusing. When you awoke today, Abeke, you could not have expected to alter the world's destiny."

"Where are you from, Zerif?" Pojalo asked.

"A traveler like me hails from all corners," Zerif replied.

"Are you a Greencloak?" Abeke felt he had the confidence of a Greencloak, if not the garment.

"I am one of the Marked, but I do not wear the green cloak. I'm affiliated with them, but I concentrate on matters relating to the Great Beasts. Have you heard talk of the battles in southern Nilo?"

"Only rumors," Pojalo said. "Foreign invaders. Our concerns of late have involved water and food."

"These rumors are the groans of a dam about to burst," Zerif said. "War will soon overtake not only all of Nilo, but all of Erdas. The Fallen Beasts are returning. Your daughter summoned one of them. This places her at the center of the conflict."

Pojalo turned toward the leopard with alarm. "We thought it looked like . . ."

"Not just looks like," Zerif corrected. "Abeke has summoned Uraza."

"How . . . ?" Soama whispered, eyes wide and frightened.

"*How* is unanswerable," Zerif said. "What she does now is the only question. I offer my assistance. You must act swiftly. This leopard will earn Abeke many enemies."

"What do you suggest?" Pojalo asked. "She is our new Rain Dancer, and is much needed."

"Her power," Zerif stated somberly, "will bring much more than rain."

Abeke frowned. This stranger Zerif clearly had plans for her, and her father seemed eager to hear him. Did he want to be rid of her? Would he act so eager if Soama had summoned this leopard?

Zerif rubbed his facial hair with two fingers. "We have much to do. First things first — you may have noticed that Uraza appears edgy. I suggest you either give the leopard the dead antelope, or else separate them."

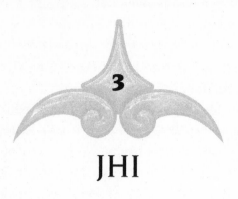

JHI

Meilin sat on a cushion before her looking glass, meticulously applying facial paint. She didn't mind letting her handmaidens prepare her for festivals or banquets. But today was important. Today she wanted to look just right. And when you wanted something done right, you did it yourself.

After finishing the accents around her eyes, Meilin inspected her handiwork. It was a work of art atop a work of art. People always remarked that she was stunning. She had never needed paint on her face to earn compliments. But now she possessed an allure beyond her natural beauty.

Anybody could get the pale base and striking lips right. But Meilin knew some tricks her handmaidens didn't—how to properly blend the blush in her cheeks, how to use gold flecks near the eyes, and how a hint of imperfection made her hair more appealing.

Meilin practiced a shy smile. Then a delighted smile, followed by a look of surprise, and finally a scowl.

Smoothing her hands over her snug silk robes, Meilin silently proclaimed her work complete.

There came a hesitant tap on the door. "Mistress," called a high voice sweetly. "Is everything all right? Can I offer any help?"

This was Kusha's polite way of informing her that the Bonding Day celebration was at a standstill. The most important people in the province were waiting on her. "I'm almost ready," Meilin answered. "I'll be out in a moment."

Meilin didn't want to make everyone wait too long, but making them wait a little would ensure that all eyes were on her. The other candidates had sampled the Nectar already. Meilin would drink it last, in the place of honor. The conventional wisdom was that the last person to drink the Nectar had the best chance of summoning a spirit animal.

As the daughter of General Teng, one of the five high commanders of the Zhongese military, Meilin had been guaranteed the last spot at the quarterly Bonding Day ceremonies since birth. As his only child, her importance was elevated further. She had no brother to steal her birthright.

Her mother had summoned a spirit animal, as had all four of Meilin's grandparents, and all eight of her great-grandparents. Her father, grandfather, and two of her great-grandfathers had been generals. The least of the others had been powerful merchants. Only the family of the emperor could claim a better pedigree.

Her father had not called a spirit animal, but even so had risen higher in the military than any of his ancestors. He was a formidable man – nobody was more cunning, or more observant, or more wrathful when crossed. Her father had told her last night that he had foreseen she would summon a spirit animal today. She didn't know whether he had visited a soothsayer or beheld the vision himself, but he had acted certain, and he was never wrong.

Meilin gathered her parasol. Made of paper and intricately painted, it was strictly ornamental. She placed it over her shoulder and took a final look in the mirror.

A heavy fist pounded the door, startling her. This was no handmaiden.

"Yes?" Meilin called.

"Are you decent?" a male voice inquired.

"Yes."

The door opened. It was General Chin, her father's closest aide, wearing his most formal uniform. How late was she?

"What is it, General?"

"My apologies for the intrusion," he said. He paused, licking his lips. He seemed perturbed, almost unsure how to continue. "I have . . . unfortunate news. The invasion of Zhong has begun. We must hurry with the ceremony, and then move out."

"Invasion?"

"Surely you know about the skirmishes in the southeast."

"Of course." Her father kept few secrets from her. But he had shared no suspicions of a serious threat.

"We just received word that they were but a prelude to a major incursion. Your father had prepared for something of the sort, but our enemies have more men and resources than even General Teng had guessed." General Chin swallowed. "The city of Shar Liwao has fallen. We are officially at war."

Meilin couldn't speak. She could hardly believe that General Chin was speaking the truth. Shar Liwao was one of the largest cities beyond the Wall, an important Zhongese port. Was this how wars started? On days that should have been happy? She suddenly felt ill, and wished she could be alone. Her father would be leaving soon. Zhong was powerful, and Erdas had no better general. He should be fine. But her father had described the uncertainties of war. A stray arrow could slay the mightiest hero. In wartime, none were truly safe.

"The entire city already fell?" Meilin had to ask.

"Yes. Reports are still coming in. The attack was lightning quick — an alliance of Zhongese rebels and foreign invaders."

"I'll skip the ceremony," Meilin said. "I can do it later."

"No, the news just arrived. The public doesn't know yet. We want to keep it that way for now. Don't mention the attack. All must appear calm and normal."

Meilin nodded. "Fine, I'll do my part. But it's an emergency. Father can go."

"He insists you drink the Nectar before he leaves."

Meilin followed General Chin out of her home. She ignored the questions of her handmaidens, who fell into step behind them. Their mansion adjoined the parade grounds, so it was not a long walk to the ceremony.

Opening her parasol, Meilin strolled down the central aisle toward the stage. Thousands of people craned to see her. General Chin strode at her side, medals gleaming.

People cheered. It seemed like an ordinary, festive occasion. These people had no clue what news was coming.

Near the stage, the bystanders were seated. More money and status meant more convenience and comfort. As Meilin approached, even the dignitaries and merchants and government officials arose and applauded.

Meilin forced the most natural smile she could manage. She gave small nods to faces she recognized. Everything felt brittle, fake. She wondered if the onlookers could see through her facade.

A boy at one side of the aisle yelled her name. It was Yenni, from her school. His father was a provincial official. He had made no secret of his affection for her, even though he was almost three years older. She gave him the shy smile. His face turned red and he grinned from ear to ear.

Meilin had never kissed a boy, although plenty had shown interest. She hated feeling like a trophy. Not only was her father rich, not only was he a popular general, but she was also attractive and refined. None of the boys actually knew her. She was just a prize, and there was no way of telling which aspect of the prize they wanted most.

She wondered how they would react if they knew her secret. Underneath the facial paint, beneath the expensive silks, she was not the dainty flower they imagined. She knew her manners. She could paint, she could serve tea, she could garden, she could recite poetry, she could sing. But her favorite pastime was hand-to-hand combat.

It had started innocently at age five. Her father was a general and a practical man. He had access to the best warriors in Zhong, and he'd wanted his daughter to learn the basics of defending herself. He had no idea how much aptitude she would demonstrate, nor how much she would enjoy it.

The training had gotten more serious each year. All in secret, she became the son her father never had. She could fight with knives, staves, and spears. She could use longbows, crossbows, and slings. But her favorite discipline involved combat using her hands and feet. A scant six weeks past her eleventh birthday, she could outmaneuver all but the greatest masters. She was slender, but strong. After she reached her adult size, she would be very formidable.

Meilin hoped that her spirit animal would augment her fighting skills. She knew that all sorts of powers could be derived from a strong relationship with a spirit animal. With the help of the right beast, good warriors became great, and great warriors became legends.

What species would benefit her most? Her father called her the Tiny Tiger. A tiger would be nice, or maybe a snow leopard. An ox could grant great strength. She tried not to set her heart on something too specific.

The crowd watched her enthusiastically. Only the top officials among them knew that war was coming. Soon they would all have much more than Nectar ceremonies to demand their attention.

When she reached the stage, Meilin folded her parasol and passed it to a handmaiden. She saw her father in the front of the crowd, dashing in his uniform, and gave a polite nod. She saw approval in his eyes. He was admiring her poise.

Many caged beasts were positioned on and around the stage, a royal menagerie including orangutans, tigers, pandas, foxes, alligators, cranes, baboons, pythons, ostriches, oxen, water buffalo, and even a pair of young elephants. Their province usually furnished a broad assortment, but this Bonding Day boasted the most variety she had seen. Her father had made sure of it.

On the stage awaited Sheyu, the leader of the local Greencloaks. He was dressed simply, and since his clouded leopard was not in sight, it was probably in its passive state. If she recalled correctly, he wore the tattoo on his chest.

Her father had mixed feelings about the Greencloaks. He respected them, but thought they had too much power and too many foreign ties. He didn't like their monopoly on the Nectar and how they used it to remain involved in everyone's affairs around the world.

Meilin was privately impressed by them. Her reasons were simple. The armies of Zhong did not invite women into their ranks, but the Greencloaks didn't fuss about such things. They measured people by their ability.

Meilin noticed a stranger on the stage. She had a foreign air about her, in both her dress and her features. Her feet were bare. She was short and thin, with that fragile look some men preferred. The feathers in her hair gave her away as an Amayan. An exotic multicolored bird stood on the stage beside her.

Sheyu beckoned Meilin. She went to him, remembering to face the crowd. It always looked amateurish when candidates turned their backs on the audience.

In a strident voice he proclaimed the ceremonial words – the same words he always said. Meilin told herself that if her father was wrong and no spirit animal appeared, she would keep composed. Her father had made his way in the world without one – she could as well.

Sheyu held a jade decanter to her lips. Meilin took a sip. The warm fluid was a bitter shock to her tongue – it took some effort to avoid gagging. Instead she forced herself to smile as she swallowed. For an unsteady moment Meilin was afraid she would choke on the taste, and then a fiery heat filled her belly. As the warmth radiated outward, her ears started ringing.

The sky was clear, but the sun dimmed. There was a brilliant flash and she was joined onstage by a black-and-white panda. It was large for the species, with disturbing silver eyes, just like Jhi on the Great Seal of Zhong.

The panda trundled over to Meilin and reared up to place its paws against her ribs. The fiery heat instantly drained away.

For a moment, Meilin felt profoundly relaxed. She was no longer playing a role in front of a crowd. She was simply herself. She basked in the warmth of the sun, and rejoiced in the gentle currents of the air around her.

Then the moment slipped away.

Meilin stared at her new spirit animal in bewilderment. A giant panda? Nobody called giant pandas, because Jhi had been a giant panda, and Jhi was a Great Beast, one of the Fallen. A large statue of Jhi stood in the far corner of the parade ground, huge and somewhat ridiculous. A panda was basically the opposite of a tiger. More silly and cute than impressive or threatening. What skills would it bestow on a fighter? The ability to eat bamboo?

The audience made no sound. Meilin found her father's eyes. He looked shocked.

The Amayan woman had come to her side. "I'm Lenori," she said quietly. "I'm here to help you."

"Are you a Greencloak?"

"I'm not wearing it, but yes. Do you realize what you've done?"

"I'm not supposed to be able to summon a panda."

"Exactly." Lenori took her hand and raised it high. "Meilin has fulfilled a prophecy that most have forgotten! Jhi the Fallen has returned to Erdas! Let us all—"

Lenori never finished her sentence, because the alarm bells started to ring, a gonging clamor reserved for emergencies. Meilin scanned the parade ground, alert. Was this connected to the invasion? That made no sense. Shar Liwao was far away, beyond the Wall of Zhong. Just as Meilin remembered to guard her expression, the great horns on the city wall sounded three times—long, low notes that warned of immediate danger.

The audience began to stir and exclaim. Aware that many eyes remained on her, Meilin held very still, trying to appear undisturbed. This was no practice exercise; the horns confirmed that. Something was horribly wrong. Did she smell smoke? It was hard to see much beyond the high walls of the parade ground.

Then the screaming began. Toward the rear of the parade ground, beyond the carefully monitored seats of the dignitaries, fighting broke out. Men and women flung off cloaks, many summoning spirit animals. Swords and axes began to cut down bystanders. As people pressed to get away, a bull charged through the crowd. A trio of arrows curved through the air to thunk down on the stage.

Meilin ignored the arrows, even though one landed close enough to kick it. The invasion was supposed to be far away, beyond the Wall! She had heard of riots in some of the outlying towns before, but nothing like that had ever happened in Jano Rion. It was a model city, one of the mightiest in all of Zhong.

With a flash, Sheyu released his spirit animal. The clouded leopard gave a savage cry. Sheyu pulled on a glove fitted with four sharp blades. With his other hand, he seized Meilin by the upper arm, giving a yank to start her moving. "They must have come for you!" he yelled.

As she stumbled after him toward the rear of the stage, Meilin craned to see the parade ground. Guards were engaging the rebels. Spear met sword, ax met shield. Some weapons found their mark. Men and women screamed. Meilin knew much about battle through her father, but until now, she had never seen anyone killed. In a few brief seconds, she saw death, and more of it than she could handle. Her last glimpse, before she jumped off the stage beside Sheyu, was of Kusha, her chief handmaiden, falling to her knees with an arrow buried in her back.

Meilin's father was there to steady her. General Chin waited at his side, along with Lenori. "Hurry," her father urged. "We must get to the tower. We need to survey the city."

The words roused her. "Right," she said, glancing back just in time to see her panda jump gracelessly from the stage. At least Jhi appeared unharmed.

Would Kusha die from that arrow? It had looked bad.

Her father ran toward the door behind the stage. Meilin followed, with Sheyu nearby. From one side, several armed rebels raced to block their retreat. A large dog ran with them, and a red panda, and an ibex with tall backswept horns.

Generals Teng and Chin drew their swords at the same time. Veering away from the door, they met the rebels violently. Pulling on a second clawed glove, Sheyu rushed to join them.

Meilin wanted to help but she was unarmed, and the enemies had weapons. She looked around frantically for a weapon, but found none.

General Chin and her father engaged the enemy with the same poise they used on the practice floor. They worked in tandem, deflecting attacks, dispatching foes, and pivoting to lend each other assistance. Sheyu and his clouded leopard ducked and weaved among the rebels, narrowly dodging attacks and efficiently slashing opponents.

Lenori dragged Meilin to the door. Jhi stayed near her. As a second group of rebels approached, Sheyu and the generals fell back.

With blood flowing freely from his shoulder, General Chin opened the door with a key. "Hurry!" he cried. The group streamed through, and General Chin locked the door behind them.

Meilin's father took off at a run, leading them along the hallway within the parade-ground wall. Meilin stayed right behind him. The thick walls muffled the tumult from the parade ground, so their footfalls echoed loudly. Glancing over her shoulder, Meilin saw Lenori's bird hopping and fluttering along. The panda brought up the rear, hurrying just enough to stay close.

Meilin could tell where her father was headed. The lookout station at the corner of the parade ground offered one of the highest vantages of Jano Rion. They would be able to see most of the city and much beyond. It was the quickest way for him to assess the situation.

As they raced along the hallway, Meilin resisted asking questions. Had they been alone it would have been different. But in mixed company, her father would volunteer information as he desired.

The soldiers at the base of the lookout tower straightened and saluted as her father drew near. He gave a quick salute back and climbed onto the lifter.

"What is that?" Lenori asked hesitantly.

"An ingenious device," Sheyu explained. "Counterweights will raise the platform to the top of the tower."

They all stepped onto the platform. The panda showed no hesitation. Meilin stared into those silver eyes as the lifter rose briskly. Despite the chaos around them, the panda appeared serene and disturbingly knowing. Meilin looked away first.

When the lifter reached the top, Meilin's father hustled them out onto the observation terrace. Soldiers with telescopes paused to salute.

"Carry on," her father said.

The ranking officer approached, but her father waved him away, preferring to use his own faculties to assess the situation. Meilin stood beside him, eyes wide, hardly believing what she was seeing.

Jano Rion was under attack. The capital of the province

and one of the largest cities in Zhong had battles raging within and without. A huge host charged the city walls, rushing across the plain like a flood. Rebels swept through clusters of defenders trying to organize themselves. Many ran alongside animals. Others rode animals. They carried swords and spears, maces and axes. Where had they come from? Why had there been no warning?

The city was burning. Black smoke billowed up from at least a dozen locations that Meilin could see. The old academy where she attended classes was aflame! That ancient building had stood for centuries. Her ancestors had studied there and now Meilin watched it fall. Fierce skirmishes came in and out of view down on the streets. Meilin craned to see, but buildings and trees blocked much of the action.

Meilin's heart squeezed as she glanced up at her father's stoic face. She could tell he was shocked, but he hid it well. Those who did not know him intimately might not recognize how deeply he was stunned. He held out a hand for a telescope. Raising it to one eye, he focused on a few areas beyond the city wall, then a few within.

"So many have spirit animals," he murmured.

General Chin had his own spyglass. "Unprecedented. There hasn't been an army like this since . . ."

"The Devourer," her father finished.

Meilin blinked. The Devourer was a legend from the past, a monster in nursery stories. Why would her father mention him at a time like this?

"Where did they all come from?" Sheyu asked. "How could that army have gotten past the Wall of Zhong without a single guard noticing?"

Meilin looked to her father. She had wanted to pose the same question. "They wear no uniforms," he said. "They didn't win through by force. They must have trickled in – perhaps over years. Many look Zhongese, but not all. It staggers me to consider the logistics involved. I would have named an attack of this scale impossible, yet here they are! The strength of Zhong is concentrated far from here, along our outer Wall. Many soldiers now travel toward Shar Liwao. But that was evidently a diversion."

"What must we do?" General Chin asked.

"We will do our duty," General Teng said. He raised his voice. "Leave us."

The other soldiers abandoned the observation terrace. Sheyu took Lenori by the arm and turned to go.

"Not you, Greencloaks," General Teng said, his voice a quiet growl. He kept a hand on Meilin's shoulder, so she knew he wanted her there as well.

Sheyu and Lenori drew closer.

Meilin watched her father. His expression made her uncomfortable. She tried to suppress the fear gnawing inside.

"Jano Rion will fall," he said plainly. "We don't have enough defenders here to resist. Lenori, you claim that Meilin has summoned Jhi herself, the living symbol of Zhong. What does it mean? What do you propose?"

"I wish to bring her to our commander," Lenori said. "Jhi is not the first of the Four Fallen to return in recent weeks. This war is coming to all of Erdas. We mean to reunite the Four Fallen and fight. It's our only chance."

Meilin felt the hand on her shoulder tighten. Her father gave a single nod. "So be it. Lenori, take my daughter. This is no place for her at present. Sheyu, please see that they embark safely from the port at Xin Kao Dai."

Sheyu placed a fist to his chest and inclined his head. "It would be my honor."

"Father, I don't want to go!" Meilin cried. "Please let me stay with you. Please let me defend our home!"

"It is not safe for you—"

"Where would I be safer than with the greatest general in all of Erdas?"

"And," he continued, holding up a hand to stay her, "you may have vital duties elsewhere." He crouched to look her straight in the eyes. "Meilin, visit with this Greencloak commander. Hear him out. If he talks sense, and the path feels true, lend the aid that duty requires. If not, seek a better path. In either instance, do not forget who you are, or where you come from."

"But—"

General Teng shook his head. "This is my will."

Meilin knew that the conversation was over. Her fate had been decided. Hot tears stung her eyes. She looked out at the army charging toward her home, then down at the ravaging traitors already at work in the parade ground. How could she run away, leaving her father to face this threat, his army divided and already half-defeated?

She glanced over at Jhi. The panda returned her gaze with understanding and perhaps a hint of pity. Was she imagining the empathy in those penetrating eyes? Meilin stared at the ground. She didn't need understanding.

She needed strength. Not only did this panda have little chance of improving her combat skills, it was also the reason the Greencloaks were taking her away.

Away from her home. Away from her father.

A clamor arose from the stairwell. An injured soldier staggered to the top of the stairs. "They're coming up! There's too many!"

Meilin's father gave a nod. "Hold them as long as you can."

The soldier turned and hobbled back down the stairs. Unseen weapons clashed. An animal screamed. Moving to the top of the stairs, General Chin drew his sword.

Meilin's father pulled the levers that lowered the lifter, then gestured to a ladder that descended the interior of the shaft. "Climb down to the first access tunnel. It should allow you to slip by the rebels. Get out of the city."

Meilin couldn't hold back her worries. "What about—"

Her father sliced his hand through the air and silenced her. "General Chin and I will confirm you reach the tunnel, then we'll make our escape." He gave his daughter a strained smile. "I won't let this rabble take me. Go."

There was no room for argument. Meilin would not shame him with further pleas or disagreements.

Meilin raised her eyes to his. "As you wish, Father."

The others were already heading down the ladder. She was mildly astonished to find Jhi capable of descending unaided. As Meilin placed her foot on the first rung, General Chin engaged his first foe. Just before her head passed down into the shaft, she saw General Chin and her father backing up, swords flashing, pressed by numerous opponents.

She kept silent. If the enemies noticed her descent, her father's efforts would be in vain. Maybe he would still get away. He was a cunning man.

With tears blurring her vision, Meilin joined the others in the cramped tunnel. Taking her hand, Sheyu led the way.

4

ESSIX

ROLLAN LOITERED ON THE CORNER BY THE APOTHECARY, keeping his back to the store. Down the cobbled street, between buildings with thick plaster walls and rounded facades, Smarty and Red were looking his way. Rollan tried to convey with his eyes that they shouldn't draw attention to him. They got the message and faced elsewhere.

An orphan since age five, Rollan knew that stealing was part of survival. Even so, he avoided it whenever possible. He had no problem with claiming leftovers, since the owners were done with them. People with money abandoned all sorts of things. Rollan had found clever ways to lay claim to unfinished meals and discarded clothing. That was salvaging, not thievery.

But his current problem would not be solved through scrounging. There was no such thing as leftover willow extract. It was too valuable. He and the boys used to have some, thanks to Hands, but it had run out. And now Digger had a terrible fever. They had wasted the precious medicine on less serious sicknesses. Had they known this was coming, they would have saved some, but it was too late.

They wouldn't be in this mess if Hands hadn't gotten arrested. The boy had a gift for pilfering, and life had been much more comfortable with him around. But Hands got greedy and started going after real valuables. The militia caught him and locked him up.

Rollan glanced over his shoulder at the apothecary. As with many businesses in town, a banner emblazoned with Essix the Falcon, patron beast of Amaya, hung over the entrance. Digger really needed help. He was burning up, and it kept getting worse. Without medicine, he could die.

Folding his arms, Rollan scowled at the ground. He didn't like to steal, but it wasn't out of deep respect for the law. Many of the profiteers in Concorba made their fortunes on the backs of the poor, taking everything they could from people who had almost nothing, and the laws protected that system. Stealing was just too risky. When kids got caught taking even the smallest thing, the penalties were harsh, especially as you got older. Plus he had his honor. His own version of it anyway – never to take from the poor, never from the sick or infirm, and always to try other alternatives first.

The other boys teased Rollan for his reluctance to pinch things. They had tried to nickname him Justice, but he had forcefully declined. Actually, he had dodged all of their attempted nicknames, which was why he was the only guy in the group without one.

No matter how he looked at it, stealing from the

apothecary would be difficult. The owner had an unfriendly reputation. His employees were vigilant, and they turned troublemakers over to the militia. Rollan had warned the others not to go after the extract. Hands could have managed it, but nobody else had a fraction of his skill.

Rollan wasn't above asking for help. Begging had been good to him. Certain bakeries and inns didn't mind handing over stale bread or other unwanted food. But times were hard and getting harder. Amaya was a young continent, much of it still untamed, and even in a big town like Concorba, if a harvest went poorly or if pirates harassed the importers, pretty soon everyone felt the squeeze. Those at the bottom of the pecking order felt it the worst.

There wasn't time to beg for enough money to buy the extract. Rollan had decided he would swipe it if he could – after all, the life of a friend outweighed some rule. But after casing the store, he didn't think success was possible. Should he try anyway?

Rollan had asked for help from everywhere that made sense. Except at the apothecary. Unlikely as that option seemed, it might be more fruitful than the alternative. Steeling himself, he went inside.

The owner, Eloy Valdez, stood behind the counter in a white apron. He had bushy gray sideburns and a receding hairline. His eyes locked on Rollan, who always drew attention when he entered a business. Even in his best clothes, he was too young and too scruffy.

Rollan walked directly to the owner. "Good afternoon, Mr. Valdez." Rollan tried on his brightest smile. He knew beneath the grime he was a handsome kid, with his dark tousled hair and tan skin, but there was a *lot* of grime.

"Hello, boy," the man replied, his gaze suspicious. "Can I help you?"

"Not me so much as a friend," Rollan said. "He has a horrible fever. This is the third day and it keeps getting worse. I'm an orphan, him too. He needs willow extract. I don't have money, but I can work hard, help tidy up, whatever you need."

Mr. Valdez made the I-wish-I-could-help-you face Rollan had seen so often. "That's an expensive remedy. And it's in short supply these days, making it more costly still."

"I don't mind putting in a lot of work," Rollan offered.

Mr. Valdez sucked air through his teeth. "You know how times are. My two assistants already take care of everything. I have no spare chores, and plenty of qualified men waiting for a vacancy. Sorry."

Rollan's cheeks burned with shame, but Digger needed him. "Maybe you could get creative? You know, to help stop a kid from dying?"

"You want charity," Mr. Valdez said knowingly. "I'm afraid I have a strict no-charity policy. Medicines are pricey. If your friend were the only soul in town who couldn't pay, I'd surely lend a hand. But endless people have desperate needs and no money. If I give you a free remedy, I should provide for all the others as well. I'd be out of business in a week."

"I won't tell anyone where it came from," Rollan promised. "You might not be able to help everyone, but you can help him. Please, Mr. Valdez. He's got nobody."

"Secrets like free willow extract don't keep,"

Mr. Valdez said. "Besides, your tale may be true, but some such stories might not be. How am I supposed to tell the difference? I can't help you. Good day."

Rollan had been dismissed. What options were left? If he returned after this, Mr. Valdez would study his every move. Stealing the extract was no longer a possibility. "How would you feel if you were alone in some alley, sick, no place to go, and everyone ignored you?"

"That's why I don't live on the streets," Mr. Valdez said. "That's why I worked hard to get where I am, and why I intend to stay here. The needs of an urchin are not my obligation."

"Hard work doesn't always get you off the streets," Rollan said, frustration surging through him. "It won't always keep you off them either. What if your store burned down?"

Mr. Valdez narrowed his eyes. "Is that a threat?"

Rollan raised both hands. "No! I just mean bad luck can strike anywhere."

"Aldo!" Mr. Valdez called. "This person needs help finding the door."

The cause was lost. Rollan decided he could stop licking Mr. Valdez's boots. "You need help finding a heart. I hope you catch something without a remedy. Something besides old age."

A large man with his sleeves rolled back over thick, hairy arms strode in from the back of the store. He came straight toward Rollan. Behind him, Smarty ducked behind the apothecary counter.

How had Smarty gotten in here? Through the back door? What was he thinking? His nickname was a joke, not a compliment. He was going to get them both busted! Rollan tried not to stare at his friend. Instead he watched Aldo approach.

"You thick?" Aldo barked. "Beat it!"

Rollan sidled toward the door, trying not to move too quickly. He needed to get out of there, but if he ran off, Smarty would get nabbed for sure.

Aldo closed the distance, seized Rollan roughly by the back of his neck, and marched him toward the doorway. "Don't let us catch you in here again," the big man warned.

"Aldo!" Mr. Valdez cried.

Looking back, Rollan saw Smarty speeding toward the back of the store.

"He took a packet of willow extract!" Mr. Valdez shouted. "Santos!"

Aldo dragged Rollan toward the rear of the store. "Get back here or your friend gets it!" the big man yelled.

Smarty never glanced back. By the time Aldo reached the back door, Smarty was out of sight.

"Santos!" Mr. Valdez cried, joining them. "Where's Santos?"

"On that errand, remember?" Aldo said.

Mr. Valdez turned furious eyes on Rollan. "All that talk about working to pay off the debt—you were setting me up while your accomplice snuck in here! Very low, even for scum."

"He did it on his own," Rollan insisted.

"Save it, kid," Aldo said. "You helped steal the goods, you'll do the time."

Rollan kicked out at Aldo's knee, but the big man took

it without a flinch. Rollan could feel the strength of the hand on his neck.

"Your next appointment is with the militia," Mr. Valdez said.

Rollan knew there was no point in arguing. At least Digger would get his remedy.

The city militia kept a line of cells in the basement of their headquarters. Mildew thrived on the damp walls, and ancient straw littered the discolored stone floor. The interior barriers were composed of iron bars, allowing the prisoners to see each other. Rollan sat on a decaying wicker mat. Men occupied three of the other cells. One man was sickly and gaunt, another had slept since Rollan arrived, and the third looked like the sort Rollan had learned to avoid. He was probably in here for something serious.

A guard had informed Rollan that he would go before a judge tomorrow. He was young enough that they might send him back to the orphanage. The thought gave him shivers. There was no worse racket than the orphanage in Concorba. The head guy lived well because he fed the kids the absolute minimum, made them work like slaves, dressed them like beggars, and never wasted resources on things like medicine. Rollan had run off for a reason. He suspected he might actually prefer prison.

A door opened, and boots clomped down the stairs. Were they bringing in a new prisoner? Rollan arose for a better look. No, the jailer was alone. He was portly with a stubbly jaw. Holding a ledger, he came to Rollan's cell. "How old are you?"

Was this a trick question? Would it benefit him more to seem older or younger? Rollan wasn't sure, so he answered honestly. "I'm twelve next month."

The man made a notation. "You're an orphan."

"Actually I'm a lost prince. If you take me back to Eura, my father will reward you."

"When did you run away from the orphanage?"

Rollan considered the question, and found no reason to fib. "I was nine."

"Have you had your Nectar?"

The question mildly surprised him. "No."

"You know what happens if you don't take the Nectar?"

"A bonding could happen naturally."

"That's right. It's against our town statutes not to drink the Nectar within three months of turning eleven."

"Good thing I'm already behind bars. Want some advice? You guys should make a law against eleven-year-olds dying because they have no medicine!"

The jailer harrumphed. "This is no game, boy."

"Does it sound like a game?" Rollan said. "Have you ever played dying-alone-of-a-fever-because-willow-bark-costs-too-much? Look, just add my lack of Nectar to my list of charges. For the record, nobody ever offered me any."

"The militia gives Nectar to any children of age who haven't received it."

"You guys deserve more medals," Rollan said.

The jailer held up a scolding finger. "If you have the potential to summon a spirit animal, it'll happen on its own by age twelve or thirteen. But do you know what could happen to you without the Nectar? The bond is a gamble. Drives some people mad, others to illness. Some die on the spot. Others are fine."

"But with the Nectar it's always stable," Rollan said.

"The Great Beasts may not have done much for us lately, but we'll always owe Ninani for the Nectar. But to benefit, you have to use it."

Rollan huffed. "What are the chances I'd call an animal? Like a hundred to one? Less?"

The jailer ignored him. "I know a Greencloak who tends to orphans. I'll send her around by and by."

The jailer turned and climbed the stairs. Rollan stretched, pivoting at the waist, then raising his hands high.

"I didn't expect a show today," said the gaunt man in the farthest cell. "What do you think you'll call?"

"Nothing," Rollan said.

"I thought the same," the gaunt man said. "I was wrong. I called a hedgehog."

"You're a Greencloak?" Rollan asked, surprised.

The gaunt man snorted. His eyes looked lost, his posture exhausted. "You see any cloak? My animal got killed. The absence left me . . . I wish I'd lost a limb instead."

An hour later, maybe two, the jailer returned with a couple of uniformed militiamen and a Greencloak. She was in her late teens and of medium height. Her face wasn't very pretty, but it was kind.

The jailer unlocked the cell gate and beckoned for Rollan to step out. One of the militiamen held a small cage with a rat inside.

Exiting the cell, Rollan nodded at the rat. "Is that a joke?"

"They say folks bond more easily if animals are present," the miltiaman said with a jeering smile. "We caught him a couple years back. He's our mascot."

"Very funny," Rollan said dryly. "Should we hunt for some spiders? Maybe a cockroach?"

"People don't bond with insects," the Greencloak said, "although there is some precedence for summoning arachnids."

"I'll bet a copper piece he calls nothing," said the prisoner who Rollan thought looked like trouble. The man patted his pockets. "Wait, two." He produced them. "Any takers?"

Nobody agreed to the bet.

"Should we do it?" Rollan suggested, breaking the awkward silence. For some kids the summoning ceremony was a big deal. They got all dressed up with their families, spectators attended, lectures were given, refreshments served. He was in a dirty jail with a rat, his guards, and his fellow prisoners. He just wanted to get it over with.

The Greencloak produced a simple flask. She uncapped it and held it out to him. "Only takes a swallow."

"That was quite a speech," Rollan said, accepting the flask. "Your talents are wasted in dank basements. You're ready to work aboveground." He took a sip. There was a restaurant that sometimes gave him sweetened cinnamon toast, his favorite treat. The Nectar tasted sort of like that, but liquefied.

Rollan wiped his lips. As the Greencloak reached for her flask, Rollan swayed. Sparks zinged through his body. What was going on? He held out the flask, but his arm felt unsteady. The Greencloak took the flask and Rollan dropped to his knees.

"What's wrong with me?" Rollan slurred.

The entire jail rumbled and the room grew dark. Or was his vision failing? A blinding light appeared, lingered for a moment, and then vanished.

A falcon had joined them in the room, large and powerful, the feathers a brownish gold with white speckles on the breast. With a flurry of wings, the raptor leaped up to Rollan's shoulder. When the claws pinched into his skin, the sparking sensation ceased. The others stared, dumbfounded.

For a moment, Rollan's eyes seemed unusually keen. He was able to see the porous textures of the stone floor and walls. He spotted a spider hiding amid the wafting cobwebs in a high corner and felt the startled moods of those around him with abnormal clarity. And then, all of a sudden, he was back to normal.

"It's a falcon!" the Greencloak marveled. "A gyrfalcon . . . with amber eyes!"

"*She's* a falcon," Rollan clarified. "She's a girl."

"How do you know that?" the jailer asked.

Rollan paused. "I just do."

"She would be female, I suppose," the Greencloak murmured. Seeming to snap out of a trance, she stared at Rollan searchingly. "How is this possible? Who are you?"

"Just some orphan," Rollan said.

"There has to be more to it than that," she muttered, half to herself.

"I'm also a criminal," Rollan volunteered. "The worst kind of criminal, actually."

"What kind is that?" the Greencloak asked.

"The kind who got caught," Rollan replied.

The Greencloak glanced at the jailer. "Put him back in his cell. I'll be back."

"The bird too?" the jailer asked.

"Naturally," the Greencloak replied. "It's his spirit animal."

"Guess it was my lucky day," mumbled the seedy prisoner. "Nobody took my bet. I get to keep my coppers."

It was not long before the jailer escorted a man to Rollan's cell. The stranger looked like some sort of foreign lord. He wore high boots, leather gauntlets, a fancy sword, and an embroidered blue cloak that Rollan guessed cost more than a team of horses. The man had a neatly trimmed beard on his chin, and gazed at Rollan with interest.

"Would you like to get out of here, Rollan?" the man asked.

"I might miss the itchy mat and the black stuff that rubs off the bars," Rollan said. "Sometimes we don't appreciate what we have until we lose it."

The man smiled, but with the hint of a sneer.

"Why isn't your cloak green?" Rollan asked.

"My name is Duke Zerif," the man said. "I work with the Greencloaks, but I'm not one of them. They send me to help with cases like yours."

"Cases like mine?"

Zerif glanced at the jailer. "Better if we converse in private. I've paid your bail."

"Fine with me," Rollan said.

The jailer opened the cell door. Rollan stepped out, the bird on his shoulder, and exited with Zerif, never glancing at the other prisoners, not saying a word to anyone. What did this guy want?

When they reached the street, Zerif looked over at him. "That is a superior bird."

"Thanks," Rollan grunted. "What now?"

"Today your new life begins," Zerif said. "We have much to discuss."

"Bail isn't a pardon. What about Mr. Valdez?"

"The charges will be dropped. I'll take care of it."

Rollan gave a slight nod. "What about the girl who gave me the Nectar? Where is she?"

Zerif flashed a cocky grin. "These matters exceed her expertise. You are no longer her assignment. Come."

The falcon gave Rollan's shoulder a brief, painful squeeze with her talons. Despite her weight, Rollan had nearly forgotten her presence. Something about the timing of the squeeze, and the way Zerif had spoken about the girl, made Rollan uneasy. "Is she all right?"

Did a trace of admiration creep into Zerif's grin? "I'm sure she's fine."

He was lying and Rollan knew it. Zerif even seemed to respect that Rollan suspected him. Rollan felt a disturbing certainty that Zerif had done something to the Greencloak. Just who was this guy?

Zerif hurried them down the street. "Where are we going?" Rollan asked.

"A quiet place to talk. Then far away from here, if you like. Have you ever yearned to see the world? That bird is your ticket."

The falcon shrieked loud enough to hurt Rollan's ears. Zerif's eyes darted between the bird and Rollan, his smile faltering a bit.

"She doesn't like you," Rollan realized.

"She's just testing her voice," Zerif answered. "I mean you no harm." Rollan would have bet two coppers that he was lying. His response had almost sounded relaxed, but Zerif was definitely acting. And he was wearing a large sword.

"What is that woman doing?" Rollan asked, pointing across the street.

As Zerif turned to look, Rollan ran. They had passed an alley, and he turned and sprinted down it. Halfway along the alley, Rollan risked a glance back and saw Zerif in pursuit, blue cloak flapping behind him. The man had jerked his sleeve back and the mark on his forearm flashed. A canine creature landed in front of him, already running. What was it? A coyote?

Rollan had hoped that the lordly stranger would be above chasing him. Apparently not. But the coyote proved that Zerif was one of the Marked. Maybe he was a Greencloak after all. Still, Rollan didn't trust him and neither did the bird. He needed to ditch him fast.

Rollan had some experience escaping down alleyways. He ran hard, and extended his hands to topple crates and rubbish bins into the path of his pursuers. In spite of his efforts, he could hear them gaining. Visions of coyote teeth and the thought of Zerif's expensive sword impelled him to run faster.

Rounding a corner, Rollan raced into another alley. He passed an occasional door, not daring to try it in case it was locked, or that whoever lay beyond might not aid him. He had learned the hard way that an orphan in flight had few friends. He glanced up, looking for a way up to the rooftops, but there was nothing in view. The man and the coyote kept gaining.

Ahead on the left, Rollan saw a fence between buildings. He jumped, grabbed the splintery top of it, and kicked one leg over. With a snarl, the coyote leaped for his dangling leg. Teeth tore through his pant leg and scraped his skin, nearly yanking him from the wall.

"Come down from there!" Zerif ordered, racing forward with his sword drawn.

Rollan rolled over the top of the fence and fell into a weedy lot with a shanty in one corner. A ragged man glared at him unwelcomingly from the shadows of his hovel. Springing to his feet, Rollan dashed across the lot. As he approached the fence on the far side, Rollan glanced back. The coyote streaked across the lot toward him, but there was no sign of Zerif. Had he tossed his spirit animal over the fence? Rollan scanned the scraggly ground ahead as he ran for something to use as a weapon but saw nothing. The coyote was closing in. He knew he would barely win the race to the fence. No way would he get up and over without getting mauled.

When Rollan reached the fence, he jumped and grabbed the top with both hands as if he meant to climb, then turned in midair to kick the coyote springing at him square in the muzzle. The blow connected cleanly, and the coyote hit the ground with a yelp. Rollan was up the fence and over before the animal had recovered.

The alley he landed in was wider. As he debated which

direction to go, Zerif shot around a far corner, running with superhuman speed. Rollan couldn't run half as fast as Zerif was moving. Zerif had gone around most of the block in the time it had taken Rollan to cross the lot. Rollan had heard stories about the powers the Marked could receive from their bonds. How could he escape from someone like that? He turned and ran the opposite way.

Racing around another corner, Rollan found himself sprinting toward a large man in a forest-green cloak astride a moose. There was no time to digest the bizarre sight. The moose barreled toward him, its massive antlers spanning almost the full width of the alley. The gray-haired man astride it had a thick build and a fleshy face framed by a bristly beard. He clutched a mace in one hand. A mail shirt jangled under his cloak.

"Out of my way, boy!" the Greencloak bellowed.

Lunging sideways, Rollan flattened himself against the wall of the alley as the moose charged past. He heard a shriek above him and the scrape of talons on metal as his bird landed on the roof.

Zerif and the coyote bolted around the corner, skidding to a halt when they saw the oncoming moose. The Greencloak gave a battle cry and raised his mace. Zerif shouldered through the first door he reached, probably the back entrance to some business. The Greencloak paused for a moment, as if about to give chase, before he rode back to Rollan.

"What name did he give?" he barked.

"That guy? Zerif."

"That much was true. Do you know him?"

"I just met him. He bailed me out of jail."

The man dismounted. "What did he tell you?"

"Not much," Rollan said. "He wanted to take me away."

"I expect he did," the man said. "We call Zerif 'the Jackal' after his spirit animal, a cunning creature native to Nilo. He works for our archenemy, the Devourer."

"The Devourer?" Rollan said. It seemed so improbable he almost choked. "Are you serious? Who are you?"

"My name is Olvan."

Rollan glanced at the huge moose and back again. No way. It couldn't be. "*The* Olvan?" he said, shocked into a whisper.

"If by that you mean the worldwide commander of the Greencloaks, then yes, *the* Olvan."

The gyrfalcon shrieked and swooped down to land on Rollan's shoulder. Rollan reached up to stroke her feathers. He paused a long moment before he spoke. "Suddenly everyone wants to be my friend. Both of you showed up so quickly. Is this about my falcon?"

"She is not *your* falcon, son. She is *the* Falcon." Olvan let the words sink in. "You have summoned Essix back into the world."

TRAINING

A BEKE SAT ON THE EDGE OF A FEATHER BED. HER ROOM HAD a carved desk, an elaborate sofa, cushioned chairs, and a mirror framed in what she thought might be real gold – all for her personal use. Everyone she encountered treated her respectfully and a servant delivered tasty meals. Her leopard had turned her into royalty.

The room gently rocked from side to side. To think such luxury was available on a ship! Abeke would not have believed it had she not seen it.

She appreciated the courteous treatment, but did not feel comfortable in the fancy room. It was too different from home. There were no familiar faces or even familiar ways.

Zerif had not joined her on the voyage. At the dock, he had explained that urgent matters called him elsewhere, and entrusted her in the care of a stranger, a boy named Shane. After everything she had lost, the extra separation had stung.

Less than a week earlier, Zerif had convinced her father that Abeke needed to leave Okaihee, not just for her personal safety, but for the good of the village. Pojalo had promptly agreed. Part of Abeke wished her father had struggled more with the decision. She could not help wondering whether he would have relinquished Soama so swiftly. With the approval of her father, Zerif had smuggled Abeke and Uraza away that same night.

Abeke regretted never talking to Chinwe before leaving. Chinwe had thought that Abeke would be the village's new Rain Dancer. They certainly needed one. In the rush to heed Zerif's advice, she had ignored the needs of her community. What if her absence meant the drought would continue? What if she had shirked her destiny? What if she had missed her chance finally to fit in?

Despite the comforts aboard the ship, Abeke missed her father and sister. Back home, they had all shared one room. They had routines, meals together, and Abeke was used to falling asleep to the sound of her father snoring. Each night on the ship, Abeke struggled to find sleep. Nothing felt familiar.

At first there had been too many new experiences to get homesick—an exciting coach ride, a busy city, a sea of endless water too salty to drink, and then a ship big enough to hold most of the people in her village. It was only after they set sail that Abeke started to feel restless. She had time to think. She had time to miss prowling the savannah. She had time to wish for familiar faces.

At least she had Uraza. Abeke rubbed the leopard's neck and the big cat purred, the vibrations tickling her palm. Uraza was not particularly affectionate, but she never rejected Abeke's stroking.

A knock came at her door. It had to be Shane. He was the other pleasant part of the voyage. He had been helping her learn to improve her connection with Uraza.

"Come in," Abeke said.

Shane opened the door. At twelve, he was only one year older than she was. He was pale, but handsome, with a sturdy build and a relaxed competence that she admired. Like her, he had a spirit animal – a wolverine.

"Ready to go to the hold?" he asked.

"I thought you'd never come," Abeke said. "I'm not used to being penned up."

He stood in the doorway, considering her. "It's hard to leave all you know behind. I had to leave my parents too. My uncle helped train me, and he's not around either."

"My mother passed away four years ago," Abeke confided. "She was the one who understood me. My father and sister . . . it was different with them. But I do miss them. I know they care for me, as I care for them."

Shane's expression softened. "People here care for you as well, Abeke. We see great potential in you. Those of us with heavy burdens find family where we can. You have your spirit animal. You'll learn to find a lot of solace there. Come."

Uraza followed them out the door. As they passed sailors and soldiers, all eyes furtively strayed to the leopard. Uraza walked with the sinuous grace of a natural predator, and nobody wanted to get too close. Even the bravest gave her plenty of space, while others changed their routes to avoid her entirely. After only four days at sea, Abeke had learned to ignore the attention.

Shane had prepared the hold for use as a training area.

Crates, bales, and barrels had been shoved aside to form a long open space. Nobody disturbed them there.

"Have you spent time talking to Uraza?" Shane asked. "Showing fondness for her?"

"Yes," Abeke said.

"Any spirit animal has unusual intelligence," he reminded her. "Yours will have much more than most. She can't talk, but that doesn't mean she won't understand."

"The Great Beasts could speak," Abeke said, passing through a door into the cargo hold. "At least they do in the stories."

"When she was a Great Beast, Uraza was larger than a horse," Shane reminded her.

"Does that mean my Uraza is a cub?" Abeke asked. The powerful leopard sure didn't look like a baby.

"Spirit animals always arrive as adults," Shane said. "Whether Uraza will grow into everything she once was is hard to guess. We'll have to wait and see."

Abeke turned to face Uraza. The leopard gazed at her, violet eyes bright.

"Can you sense her mood?" Shane asked.

"I don't know," Abeke said, staring hard. "Interested, maybe?"

"That seems likely," Shane said. "The more you practice, the better you'll perceive her emotions. That's the first step to borrowing her energy in times of need."

"What about the passive state?" Abeke had always been impressed by Chinwe's ability to change her wildebeest into a tattoo on her leg.

"That is more up to Uraza than to you," Shane said. "You must gain her trust. She enters her passive state voluntarily, but she can't emerge until you release her."

"You keep your wolverine dormant?" Abeke asked. Once, at her pleading, he had bashfully shown her the hint of a mark high on his chest.

"Most of the time. Renneg is great in a fight, but doesn't play well with others. When Uraza consents, you'll get to pick where the mark will go. Many choose their arms or the back of the hand. It's convenient."

Abeke had only seen the wolverine once, when they were boarding the ship. It was compact, but looked vicious.

Shane held up a short wooden stick. "We did enough archery yesterday. You're good, but I didn't sense Uraza making you any better. I thought today we should try something more strenuous. We'll pretend this is a knife. All you have to do is stab me."

He handed Abeke the stick. Abeke went and knelt before Uraza. The leopard lounged on the floor, body curled, head up, long tail swishing languidly. Abeke took in the spotted perfection of her pelt, the black around her vibrant eyes, and the muscular power of her sleek body. How could such a strong, wild creature be her companion? Uraza gazed at her, unblinking.

Abeke gently touched one of her paws. "We're a team now. Like it or not, we're both far from home, but at least we have each other. I can tell you don't love this ship. Neither do I. But it's just taking us someplace where we can be outside again. I really do like you—you're quiet, you're not pushy, and we come from the same place. I want to learn to work together."

Uraza purred and Abeke fluttered inside. Was it her

imagination, or had they begun to connect? It was difficult to be sure.

Abeke turned to face Shane.

"Whenever you're ready," he invited.

Abeke shuffled forward, the stick held in front of her. Back home, she had used a spear at times, and had practiced a lot with a bow. She knew little about fighting with a knife.

This didn't seem like an effective way to confront a larger, more experienced opponent. She would never approach somebody like Shane openly. Her only chance would be to strike from behind, attack out of hiding. With surprise on her side, she'd have much better odds of succeeding.

But this was just practice. She needed to fight according to Shane's guidelines. Maybe there was something predatory in Uraza that would amplify her efforts.

As Abeke closed in, she tried a quick stab. Shane pivoted away, slapping her wrist. Three more stabs led to three more slaps. She felt no assistance from Uraza. "This is pointless," Abeke groaned, relaxing her stance.

"You just need—"

She lunged and stabbed hard, hoping to catch him off guard. Shane dodged her attack and seized her wrist. For a moment they struggled. Abeke silently asked Uraza for help. Shane pried the stick from her fingers and touched it to her belly.

"Good try," he said. "You almost caught me napping."

"I would never attack you like this in real life," Abeke said. "I'd sneak up on you."

Shane nodded. "That would be smarter. And more suited to how a leopard would hunt. Tell you what—I'll go to the far side of the hold and stand with my back to you. I won't turn unless I hear something suspicious. Deal?"

Abeke nodded. This new game would play to her more proven abilities.

Shane returned the stick to her and trotted to the far side of the room. Staying low, her pretend knife ready, Abeke crept forward. Step by step she drew nearer.

"Are you moving yet?" Shane asked, facing away from her. "If so, you're good at it. If not, hurry up—we don't have all day."

Abeke fought against a smile. She knew that she was a skilled stalker, and it was nice to hear Shane recognize it. Glancing over her shoulder, she found the leopard watching attentively, her posture more alert than earlier.

The door near Shane burst open and a figure raced toward him. Robed in black, face covered, the attacker held a curved sword ready. Shane ducked a swipe of the sword and grappled with the intruder.

"Run, Abeke!" Shane shouted. "It's an assassin. Fetch the captain!"

The assassin was bigger than Shane. They wrestled for control of the sword.

Abeke found herself in a low crouch, both unfamiliar and instinctive. A foreign energy blazed into her muscles— every fiber seemed taut and ready to release. Her senses had never felt so keen. She heard the subtle creak of the timbers as the ship rocked gently to the right. She could smell the attacker, a full-grown man, and could distinguish easily between him and Shane. Her vision was enhanced as well, sharpened. No part of her intended to heed Shane's instruction to run.

Her heart swelled with courage. And she sprang.

Although several paces from Shane, Abeke closed the distance with a single leap. Hurtling through the air, she lashed out with one leg and kicked the attacker in the arm. He spun to one knee and his sword flew free, clattering across the plank floor. The man rose to his feet with a vicious uppercut that Abeke evaded almost without thought. He backed off a step or two, one hand up, ready for combat, the other flopping useless at his side. Abeke leaped forward and kicked him in the ribs, her foot crashing through his attempt to block it. The blow landed with enough force to send the assassin flying into the wall. He slumped facedown.

Her instincts screamed to finish the job, but before Abeke could close in, she felt a firm hand on her shoulder. "No, Abeke! No more! It was pretend. He was acting."

She slipped out of her heightened state and glared at Shane. "Pretend?"

Uraza gave an angry growl, the first Abeke had heard from the leopard.

"I wanted to see how you would perform under pressure," Shane explained. "It worked, Abeke. That was incredible! Many of the Marked train their entire lives without ever attacking like that."

Trembling with unreleased energy, Abeke struggled to calm herself. The praise did not escape her notice, but it was hard to embrace it when she felt so stunned. "You got a true response through trickery," she said. "What you just did to us was a betrayal."

"I-I'm sorry." Shane's smile fell. His earlier excitement gave way to embarrassment. "Really. I was trying to help. It was a training technique. I didn't know you'd see it this way."

"Never again," Abeke said, struggling to calm herself, "or the next time you're in trouble, we will let the attackers have you."

"Agreed." Shane ran a hand through his hair. "You're right, it was unfair to you and to Uraza. It won't happen again."

Abeke felt some of the tension leave her. She nodded toward the fallen assailant. "Is he all right?"

Shane crouched beside him and felt his neck. "He's unconscious. He'll live." He shook his head. "Honestly, I couldn't imagine you would have been able to take out a trained, full-grown opponent. Let me take care of this. You know the way back to your cabin."

Abeke turned and found Uraza facing her, having approached silently. Now there was no doubt about the wordless understanding. Abeke held out her arm. With a searing pain and a brief flash, Uraza leaped to become a blaze of black just below her elbow.

SUNSET TOWER

ROLLAN STOOD WITH HIS HEAD TIPPED BACK, USING ONE hand to shield his eyes from the sun as he followed the flight of his falcon. Essix turned in two wide circles, soaring higher than the tallest spire of the Greencloak fortress.

The grass came up to Rollan's knees. Inside Sunset Tower, they had training rooms and spacious courtyards, but he preferred spending time outside the walls. Too many people inside the fortress stared at him, some with doubt, others expectantly. Either reaction unsettled him.

Besides, it was prettier outside. Wilderness had surrounded Concorba at a distance, but he rarely ever saw it. There were a few parks in town, some weedy lots, and the muddy banks of Sipimiss River, but the port city was mostly a place of commerce. He had occasionally seen farmland beyond the town boundaries, but nothing like this—not big hills, not woods, not wild meadows.

An imposing collection of bulky structures enclosed by tall walls of heavy stone, Sunset Tower was not the main Amayan stronghold of the Greencloaks. Rather, it served as the westernmost Greencloak outpost in Northern Amaya. Any farther west led to untamed land controlled mostly by beasts and the Amayan tribes.

Rollan whistled. "Essix, to me!"

The bird continued to glide on lofty breezes.

"Essix, come!"

The falcon drifted through another lazy turn.

"*Get down here!* How hard is it to follow simple instructions? The dimmest kid I know can do that much!"

Bad move. Essix now seemed to be flying farther away from him on purpose. Rollan took a calming breath. He had already learned that shouting angry words would keep the bird in the sky all day. "Please, Essix," he called more gently. "Olvan wants us to learn to work as one."

The falcon tucked her wings and plunged toward him. He held up a protected hand, the large brown glove a gift from Olvan. After arrowing down with blinding speed, Essix spread her wings at the last moment to slow her descent and alighted on his forearm.

"Good girl," Rollan said, stroking her feathers. "Want to try the passive state? Want to become a mark on my arm?"

Rollan needed no comprehension of bird speech to recognize that her piercing cry meant absolutely not. Rollan gritted his teeth but kept petting her. "Come on, Essix. You don't want us to look useless when the others get here. Let's show them what we can do."

The falcon cocked her head to stare at him with one amber eye. Her feathers ruffled up, but she made no further sound.

"Hey, it doesn't just reflect on me," Rollan said. "It makes you look bad too."

Behind him, a horn sounded. Another horn answered. The Greencloaks at Sunset Tower liked to announce their comings and goings with horns.

"That probably means they're here," Rollan said.

Essix hopped to his shoulder.

Yesterday, Olvan had informed Rollan that two of the other three Fallen Beasts were on their way to Sunset Tower with their bonded partners. He explained that after they arrived, Rollan would learn more about what was needed from him. There was always one reason or another to delay a full explanation.

Rollan wondered if the other kids had already taken the Greencloak vows. Olvan said that the vows meant a lifetime commitment to defending Erdas and standing united with the other Greencloaks. In return, Rollan would receive help developing his relationship with Essix, he would be given duty and purpose, and he would never want for food, shelter, or fellowship.

Rollan wasn't sure he bought it. The return of the Four Fallen was supposed to be a really big deal, but Olvan refused to say what they were actually meant to do. How long did Olvan expect him to wait?

Now that Essix had freed Rollan from a life of poverty, he questioned whether he wanted to tie himself down. He had never enjoyed taking orders. People with authority tended to abuse it. With Essix on his shoulder, who knew what options awaited? It was possible that joining the Greencloaks would prove to be his best opportunity, especially if he had become a target of people like Zerif. Then again, Rollan hadn't had time to explore all of the alternatives. Instead of turning down Olvan, Rollan asked for time to think it over. That had been three days ago.

As Rollan tromped through the tall grass toward the gate of Sunset Tower, a grim Greencloak astride a mighty horse rode into view. A girl walked beside the Greencloak on one side and a boy on the other. A panda ambled beside the girl, and a large wolf loped beside the boy. They were all headed for Rollan, so he picked up his pace. He knew the panda and wolf must be two of the other Fallen, Jhi and Briggan.

The Greencloak dismounted when he drew near, and Rollan sized him up. He was the sort of stranger Rollan would have avoided on the streets of Concorba.

The boy had blond hair and wore a green cloak, meaning he had taken the vows. Although he was average height for his age, he seemed young. He had a friendly, open face – the sort of face that hadn't figured out what life was like yet. The girl was striking. She had sparkling eyes and a shy smile that stopped Rollan in his tracks. A faint response in her expression told Rollan that she appreciated his reaction, and he realized that her shy smile was practiced. Judging by her outfit and her features, she came from Zhong, which made sense, given her spirit animal. Rollan had never seen a real panda. Or a wolf. His only exposure to such creatures came from the Widow Renata, who used to visit the orphanage and read them picture books about the Great Beasts.

"I'm Tarik," the Greencloak said. "I take it you're Rollan?"

"I was trying to keep a low profile," Rollan said. "How could you tell? It was the falcon, wasn't it?"

"Meilin, Conor, I would like you to meet Rollan," Tarik

said. "He was born and raised here in Amaya. Just as you two summoned Jhi and Briggan, he called Essix."

The wolf padded forward and the falcon fluttered down to stand before it. The panda moved in close as well, and Essix gave a soft screech. The three animals cautiously investigated each other.

"Do they remember?" Meilin asked, speaking Common. She had a nice voice. It matched her appearance.

"Perhaps," Tarik said. "It's difficult to pinpoint how much of their former lives they recall. Much of it might be instinct at this stage."

"What about the fourth Fallen Beast?" Rollan asked. "Uraza."

Tarik scowled. "Somebody got to Uraza and her new partner before us, much as Zerif attempted with you. The girl is named Abeke. We don't know her present location, but we won't rest until we find her. Lenori believes that she and Uraza are still alive. The challenge will be finding them."

"Is Lenori how you found us?" Conor asked.

Tarik nodded. "Lenori is the most gifted visionary of all the Greencloaks. Thanks to her unique foresight, we suspected the Four Fallen were returning."

"Her powers can't be entirely unique," Rollan pointed out. "Not if somebody beat you to the girl in Nilo."

"If Uraza is currently lost," Meilin said, "then the three of us must represent the Four Fallen. Aren't we supposed to learn what's going on, now that we're together?"

"That information is Olvan's to share," Tarik told her. "You already know that we want you to join the Greencloaks and help us preserve Erdas."

"From the Devourer?" Rollan asked, not hiding his skepticism.

Tarik seemed momentarily startled by this question. "Who mentioned the Devourer?"

"This guy I met," Rollan said. "He was riding a moose."

"We're still not positive who we're up against. If it isn't the Devourer himself, it's somebody very much like him. It shouldn't be long before Olvan explains why we need your help. For the moment, you three should seize this chance to get better acquainted. You'll see a lot of each other in the coming days. I'll ride ahead to announce our arrival."

"Get ready to be stared at," Rollan warned the others as Tarik rode away. "It's all people have done since I arrived. At first I worried I had food on my face."

"People tend to stare at newcomers," Meilin said. "Especially important ones."

"I guess our animals make us important," Conor said, sounding uncertain whether he believed it.

The conversation died out. Conor looked uneasy.

Rollan sized up the other two and their animals. Briggan was the most impressive beast. Rollan knew some people back in Concorba he would love to scare with a wolf like that. The panda just sat pawing at the grass. Conor seemed shy. Meilin acted uninterested.

"Judging by your clothes, I take it you're rich," Rollan said to her.

"Wealth is relative," she replied with a cold look. "The emperor has much more treasure than my father."

Rollan chuckled. "If the Zhongese emperor is your example of someone richer than you, you have to be loaded."

"My father is a general and there are also successful merchants in my bloodline."

"Yep, rich," Rollan said. "What about you, Conor? Do you have a family or a bloodline?"

Conor blushed a little, glancing at Meilin. "A family. We have bloodlines, I guess, but we don't use that word. We're shepherds. I got stuck as a servant for a time, but I always preferred the outdoors."

"And I'm an orphan," Rollan said bluntly. "I'm only here because Essix was my ticket out of jail."

"Jail!" Conor exclaimed. "What did you do?"

Rollan checked to make sure they were both listening closely, then leaned in. "Actually, I was innocent – not that I had any proof. I was arrested for stealing medicine from an apothecary."

"Were you sick?" Conor asked.

"A friend had a bad fever. But I didn't swipe the medicine. Another friend did. I was around when it happened, so they assumed I was in on it."

"Which is the lie?" Meilin asked. "That you were in jail, or that you were there for stealing medicine?"

Rollan shrugged. "You got me. I'm actually Olvan's son. He's having me spy on you."

Meilin didn't challenge him further, but Rollan could tell she didn't trust him. Maybe she wasn't completely stupid. It was a pretty far-fetched story. Plus she hadn't accepted a green cloak yet.

Conor peered over his shoulder at Sunset Tower. "What do you think they want us to do?"

"Maybe you should have asked before you put on the cloak," Rollan suggested.

"I expect they'll want us as soldiers," Meilin said. "Leaders, probably. The war has already begun."

"I bet they want us as mascots," Rollan said. "They'll probably add me to the Amayan flag."

Conor laughed, blushing slightly. "Can you imagine? As if all the attention didn't make me uncomfortable enough."

"This is a poor hour for humor," Meilin snapped, her eyes blazing. "Zhong is under heavy attack. The Greencloaks smuggled me away as my father fought to defend our city. I still haven't heard whether he lived or died! Whatever they have planned for us better be good."

Rollan eyed her warily. "I'm not sure how helpful I'll be," Rollan said. "Do you two have any tips about the animals? I can hardly get Essix to do anything."

"I've been trying with Briggan," Conor said, crouching to pet his wolf. "He can be stubborn. The more we've gotten to know each other, the better it's become. Tarik told me that eventually we can get powers from them."

Rollan glanced at Meilin and her panda. "What's your power going to be? Cuddling?"

Meilin's face was pure ice. For a moment her lips trembled, but after that the anger only touched her eyes. She held out her arm and in a flash Jhi became a design on the back of her hand. She turned and stormed away.

"See," Rollan called. "Like that! How did you figure that out?"

"Too late," Conor said quietly. "I haven't known Meilin long, but I can tell she has a temper."

"Can you do that too?" Rollan asked. "The tattoo thing?"

"Not yet," Conor said.

Rollan stroked Essix. "At least we're not the only slow learners."

Sunset Tower was dark and still as Rollan crept out of his room. He paused, listening, ready with answers if he was challenged by a watchman: He couldn't sleep; he needed a snack.

But no challenge came.

Peering back into his room, Rollan saw Essix roosting near the window, head tucked in sleep. He eased the door closed. The open window would allow the falcon to catch up with him. The bird might not approve of his decision, which was why he hadn't tried to explain, but she would follow. They were linked now.

Along the hallway, small oil lamps trimmed to a slow burn provided dim light. Moving down the corridor, Rollan felt the alert guilt of a trespasser. The late hour meant he might not encounter anyone, but if he did, he knew it would look extra suspicious. The farther he deviated from the path to the kitchen, the more conspicuous he felt. How could he answer why he was heading for the castle gate fully dressed with a satchel? Why did he need a snack when his satchel was crammed with stolen food? His responses sounded so unlikely: He couldn't relax; he felt confined; he needed some fresh air. Anyone with half a brain would guess the truth.

He was running away.

The thought produced a stab of remorse, which he tried to shrug off. Had he ever asked to come here? Olvan had promised to protect him from Zerif, but who would protect him from Olvan? Rollan knew that, in theory, he was a guest of the Greencloaks, but he was starting to feel more like a prisoner. Sure, it was mostly smiles and politeness now. But the Greencloaks' expectations were his chains. How long would the friendliness last if he quit following orders? How long would it last if they caught him tonight?

He and the others had returned to the fortress earlier to – once again – the weight of the promised stares. The Greencloaks helped Conor and Meilin get settled, but no additional information was forthcoming. Rollan had asked more questions, but – once again – they were deflected. That evening, Rollan decided he had waited for specifics long enough. The more time he stayed, the clearer it became that the Greencloaks would settle for nothing less than a lifelong commitment, so they could benefit from his falcon. With Conor and Meilin here, the pressure on him would only increase. Each day he stayed implied that he meant to commit. If he wanted to get away, the time to act was now.

Besides the big gate, Rollan had seen three minor gates in the outer wall. All were heavily reinforced and disguised from the outside. As far as he could tell, they only opened from within. Over the past week he had tried all of them. He knew which one he would use tonight.

Rollan heard the tones of a distant conversation up ahead and froze. He couldn't distinguish words, but the blurry murmuring had no urgency to it. Apparently, guards were covering the main door to the courtyard, chatting to pass the time. That was no obstacle. Too many doors led from the main building out to the courtyard for them all to be guarded. There was no war here in Amaya, and people had to sleep.

Stepping lightly but swiftly, Rollan advanced along a narrow corridor toward another door that would lead outside. From up ahead a voice floated his way. "Come on, Briggan! You don't want food; you don't want to go outside – can't this wait until morning?"

It was Conor! What was he doing up? Rollan slipped down a side corridor, unsure where it led. He went around a corner and paused to listen. He could barely hear the wolf, but Conor was making no effort to walk quietly. They were coming his way!

Moving faster, Rollan took a couple other turns before the hall ended at a locked door. Breathing softly, he listened as Conor and the wolf got nearer and nearer. Surely they would turn a different direction! Why would they come down a dead end?

Unless the wolf was tracking him.

Rollan folded his arms and leaned against the wall, hoping he could sell the idea that he was just hanging around the castle. At this hour, it didn't seem very believable, but Conor didn't give the impression that he was a genius.

Conor came into view with Briggan. The wolf stopped, staring at Rollan. Looking rumpled and tired, Conor squinted. "Rollan? What are you doing here?"

"Couldn't sleep," Rollan said. "I was exploring. Why are you up so late?"

Conor yawned and stretched. "I was trying to sleep, but Briggan kept pawing the door."

Rollan looked at the wolf. It sat back, mouth open, tongue dangling.

Conor wrinkled his nose. "Why hang out here? Are you up to something?"

"Fine," Rollan said, as if about to reluctantly admit the truth. "Essix went out flying but hasn't returned. I want to make sure she's all right."

"So you came here. To a dead end," Conor clarified.

"I lost my way."

"So you stood against a door."

Rollan thought fast. Maybe Conor wasn't so dim, after all. "I heard you coming and got embarrassed. I didn't want to seem lost. I really am concerned about Essix."

Conor frowned. "If you're worried, we should tell Olvan. I'm sure he has lots of people who can help us find Essix."

Rollan hesitated. It had been a feeble excuse, but better than pretending he thought the kitchen was on this side of the castle. "You're right. Why don't you and Briggan go tell Olvan? I want to get started on my own just in case."

Conor glanced at the satchel. "What's in the bag?"

"Falcon food. You know . . . as bait."

Conor gave him a look. "Big bag for falcon food."

Rollan sighed and gave up. "Look, don't get Olvan. Essix is fine. I'm just . . . thinking about a change of scenery."

"You're running away?" Conor blurted incredulously. Briggan cocked his head.

"I'm escaping," Rollan clarified.

"You're not a prisoner," Conor said.

"I'm not so sure!" Rollan replied. "You think they'd let me go? Just wander off with Essix?"

Conor paused. "Yeah, if you insisted."

"How would you know? You signed up as soon as they dangled a cloak in front of you."

Conor shifted. "I signed up after I learned that I had summoned Briggan," he replied defensively. "I never asked for my own Great Beast, but it happened, and now the Greencloaks need my help to protect the world."

"From what?" Rollan scoffed. "They still haven't explained! Not really. We hear there's a war in Zhong. They whisper about the Devourer. People I've never met look at me hopefully, and I have no idea what they expect. Even if my falcon really is the same Essix from the old stories, what are we supposed to do about a war? In the stories Essix was huge and could talk. This Essix hardly seems to like me!"

"I wonder why," Conor said. Briggan gave his head a quick shake. Was the wolf laughing at them?

"Watch it, sheep boy." Rollan bristled. "You might like being herded, but that isn't my style."

"Yeah, well, at least I don't run away the second I get scared," Conor replied with sputtering anger. "You think this isn't hard for me? You think I don't have doubts too? You think I want to be stuck in some castle across the sea from my home? Go ahead and call me sheep boy any time you want. Herding sheep takes a lot more courage and know-how than sneaking away in the night!"

Rollan found himself temporarily at a loss for words. If Conor was working with the Greencloaks in spite of his own doubts, because he thought it was the right thing to do, well, there wasn't much fault to find in that. Not that he had to admit it.

"I just need some space," Rollan said softly, choosing to fight honesty with honesty. "How am I supposed to think this through while surrounded by Greencloaks? Every meal I eat, every hand I shake, feels like pressure to join them. How am I supposed to make my own choice? The Greencloaks probably aren't bad folks. But I'm not sure their interest in me goes one inch beyond the falcon. That means they're using me and that makes me cautious."

"I hear you," Conor said. "Nobody paid much mind to me either, until Briggan came along. Then I was suddenly the center of attention."

"Doesn't that make you question their motives?"

Conor gave a little nod and Briggan stared expectantly at him. "Maybe. But I'm convinced that they're trying to defend Erdas. They need Briggan, so they need me too. Besides, Briggan seems to trust them."

The wolf wagged his tail and began to pace.

Rollan glanced at the corridor behind Conor. "Whatever I choose, I guess I blew my escape tonight. You going to turn me in?"

"You haven't done anything," Conor replied, meeting Rollan's eyes steadily.

Rollan lowered his head and rubbed his eyebrows with his knuckles. "I guess I could wait around to hear the specifics."

"You could probably make a better choice that way," Conor pointed out.

"Meanwhile, they'll have the chance to keep reeling me in," Rollan said. "I won't let them force me into this. I don't care if it gets awkward. I don't even care if they lock me up. Actually, if they lock me up, I'll know I made the right call."

Conor extended his arms and opened his mouth in a jaw-cracking yawn. "I'm glad you might stick around for now. I'd hate to be left alone with Meilin."

Rollan smirked. "Does she scare you?"

Conor shrugged. "I've got two brothers. I don't know the first thing about girls."

"I hear they like flowers."

"If you say so." Conor turned and patted the side of his leg. "Come on, Briggan, let's get back to bed. Good night, Rollan."

"Night." He watched until Conor walked out of sight. Then Rollan reconsidered his options. He supposed he could still make his escape. But the mood had left him.

Rollan started back toward his room. His secret departure may have been compromised, but all was not lost. He could always steal away some other night.

7

TEAMWORK

ON HER WAY TO THE TRAINING ROOM, ALMOST EVERY single person Meilin passed stared at her. Some covertly, some unashamedly gawking. Conversations stopped in mid-sentence when she came into view, and once she passed, whispers followed her. The few who didn't stare sent her careful glances or self-conscious waves and nods, which were almost more telling. Rollan was right. The Greencloaks had heavy expectations of her.

Meilin entered the wide and airy room and found Conor waiting with his wolf. The training area looked almost too large—much bigger than the practice space she had used with the masters back home. She guessed the vaulted ceiling was meant for Greencloaks with winged beasts.

"Glad to see you," Conor said, rubbing his arm self-consciously. "I was starting to worry I'd come to the wrong place."

"I got a message with my breakfast," Meilin said. "They asked me to report here with Jhi as soon as I finished."

Conor nodded. "Me too. I could hardly eat after the note. I can't, um, I don't know my letters very well, so I had to get help to read it." Conor reddened. "Did it sound like a test to you?"

"Some kind of assessment."

Conor glanced at Briggan, then back at Meilin. "I guess Jhi is on your hand?"

"She seems to prefer it much of the time."

Conor nodded, then seemed very aware that he had run out of things to say. Crouching, he stroked Briggan. Meilin watched him avoid her gaze. He was a simple boy, baseborn, uneducated, yet in one important way he was her peer—he had summoned one of the Four Fallen. Why him? Could it be random chance? If so, why her? Would random chance select someone as prepared for leadership as herself?

Rollan entered the room, the falcon on his shoulder. "Am I late?"

Conor looked up, relief stamped on his face. "Glad you're here."

Some quiet understanding passed between them. What had she missed? Had they discussed her in private? With Zhong under attack, she didn't want to spend any time worrying about such trivial things—but she couldn't help it, and that annoyed her.

"Nobody else has shown up yet?" Rollan asked.

"Not yet," Conor said.

Rollan scanned the weapons held in racks against the walls: swords, scimitars, knives, spears, polearms, axes, staves, and clubs. "Are we going to fight to the death?"

"Nothing that exciting," Tarik said, entering the room

with two other men and a woman. All three wore green cloaks and were new to Meilin. They paid rapt attention to Essix and Briggan. "We evaluate all new recruits to gauge their abilities."

Rollan looked at the other Greencloaks. "Who are your friends?"

"Observers," Tarik answered calmly. "They'll assist you as needed. Pay them little mind. I just want to put each of you through a few exercises."

"Finally," Rollan grumbled, "somebody to stare at us."

The two men crossed to Conor and Rollan. The woman approached Meilin. She was thick but not flabby, and had a no-nonsense look about her.

"Meilin, could you produce Jhi?" Tarik asked.

Meilin focused her attention on the simple tattoo on the back of her hand. When her interest was elsewhere, she hardly noticed the mark. But now she could perceive warmth beneath the image, a vague presence. She mentally called to Jhi, imagined a door opening, and then with a flash the tattoo vanished and Jhi appeared.

"Well done," Tarik complimented. "Some who have newly learned to use the passive state struggle to release their animals. You did that swiftly, which is important. While passive, your spirit animal cannot aid you."

Meilin gave a nod and a modest smile. Although accustomed to praise, she was not entirely immune to its effects. She noticed the boys, particularly Rollan, watching her enviously. Keeping her eyes on Tarik, she pretended not to care.

"Please allow your escorts to blindfold you," Tarik instructed. "We're going to test your awareness of your spirit animals without the aid of sight."

Meilin held still as the woman placed a blindfold over her eyes.

"Do you guys fight a lot with your eyes closed?" Rollan asked.

Meilin had been thinking the same thing, but she never would have said it.

"This will simulate a situation where your spirit animal is out of view," Tarik explained patiently, as if the question had not been meant to rattle him. "Relax and follow instructions."

A hand took Meilin by the elbow and led her several paces. With great care, she retained a sense of where she stood in the room. She waited for perhaps a minute.

"The animals have all changed position," Tarik announced. "I now challenge each of you to point out the location of your animal. I respectfully ask the animals to keep silent."

Meilin strained her senses but could neither hear nor smell anything. She thought about the vague presence she could feel beneath the tattoo when Jhi was in her dormant state, and tried to sense a similar presence around her. Nothing.

"Good, Conor. Very close," Tarik said.

Meilin kept her face composed but felt disappointed. Could Conor have a stronger connection to his spirit animal than she had to hers? He couldn't even use the passive state! Maybe he had made a lucky guess.

"I'm sorry, Rollan, you're way off," Tarik said. "But good job, Conor. Briggan is moving and you're tracking him well."

Meilin silently ordered Jhi to make herself known.

From the start, Jhi had obeyed her requests, but Meilin still felt nothing.

"Meilin," Tarik said, "if you're unsure, rely on your instincts."

She didn't want to point randomly, but maybe Tarik was giving her a hint. Maybe her awareness of her creature was something felt only at an instinctive level. That might explain why Conor was good at it – she doubted his problem would be too much thought.

Following a whim, Meilin extended a finger to the right.

"Not even close, Meilin," Tarik said, with a touch of humor in his tone.

Meilin pointed to the left.

"Better, but still far off," Tarik reported.

Meilin had to work to keep her expression neutral. What sort of absurd contest was this? She silently *demanded* for Jhi to reveal herself. Once again, she sensed nothing.

"Not bad, Rollan," Tarik said. "Not good, but you're doing too well for it to only be chance. Conor, you're a natural at this."

Meilin tried not to feel flustered. She had never attempted to sense Jhi like this. Had the boys practiced? Probably.

"Care to try one more time, Meilin?" Tarik asked.

She pulled off her blindfold. "I feel nothing." She looked to where Jhi strolled near one wall of the training area, led by an escort.

"It's not unusual," Tarik told her.

Meilin watched Conor's finger follow Briggan, staying on the animal even when the wolf reversed direction. Essix flew around overhead. Rollan seemed to be able to identify which half of the room the bird was in, but not much else.

"How can I improve?" Meilin asked.

"You can already call Jhi to her passive state," Tarik acknowledged, "so earning the trust of your beast does not seem to be the problem. I imagine it will just take time to strengthen your connection. Part of that includes your receptiveness to her."

Meilin nodded. Jhi always obeyed her orders, so what had gone wrong? Perhaps Tarik was right. Perhaps the panda was trying. Meilin frowned. Maybe she was the one unable to receive the cues. Aside from Jhi's obedience, they weren't very close. What would it take? Deep affection? Mutual understanding? It was hard to respect such a docile, slow animal. But Jhi was her spirit animal. There would be no other. Meilin knew she had to make it work.

"You may remove your blindfolds," Tarik invited.

Meilin glanced at the weapons on the walls. The wooden swords were obviously practice gear. Many of the arms looked real, though some of them could be blunted. With or without help from Jhi, Meilin expected she could dominate either of the boys in just about any form of combat. Such a demonstration would be satisfying, but would it be wise? Her father had always told her to keep her abilities private so she could surprise adversaries in times of need.

"Next we'll try a physical exercise," Tarik announced. "All three of you will go to the far wall." He indicated the wall he meant. "You'll run across the room and touch this other wall as high as you can, then run back and strike the suspended bag with all your might. Ask your animals to enhance your efforts in any way they can."

Meilin surveyed the canvas bag hanging from a beam near the far wall. Suspended by a chain, the bulging sack was taller than her and looked heavy.

"Will we do it at the same time?" Meilin asked.

"Yes," Tarik said. "The first to reach the bag will strike it first, and so forth. We'll evaluate your speed, the height of your leap, and the force with which you hit the bag. Go ahead and take a moment with your animals."

Meilin approached Jhi. The panda sat on her hind legs and watched her serenely. Jhi licked one of her paws. The relaxed attitude did little to boost Meilin's confidence.

"Can you help me with this?" Meilin asked. "Can you give me extra speed? Extra energy? I've never felt that from you. This might be a good time to start."

The panda cocked her head as if mildly perplexed.

"Look," Meilin whispered harshly. "Every minute we are stuck here in training is another minute that my father and his army have to struggle without us. I know you have power—you're a Great Beast. So I need you to help me, because every delay helps our enemy. Do you understand? We're not playing a game here. We are at war."

Did Meilin sense a degree of understanding in that unblinking silver gaze? Or was it imagined?

The boys were heading to the wall, so Meilin trotted to join them. Her body was in good condition. Even though it had been a few weeks since a formal training session with the masters, she had engaged in regular routines while traveling to maintain her reflexes and endurance.

The boys were taller, but she wasn't slow, and she knew how to deliver vicious blows.

Briggan paced along one of the side walls, watching the three with a predator's intensity. Essix flew up to roost on the beam above the suspended bag. Jhi sat where Meilin had left her, looking on silently.

Rollan smirked at her. "Did you have to run much in your palace?"

"I didn't live in a palace," Meilin replied. It was true, although she realized her home would probably look like a palace to Rollan or Conor. Assuming it still stood.

"I run fine," Conor volunteered. "I haven't done it much lately. How about you, Rollan?"

"Orphans have to run well," he replied. "A slow orphan ends up in jail."

"Weren't you just in jail?" Meilin asked innocently.

"Are you ready?" Tarik called.

One Greencloak observer stood by them against the starting wall. Another was positioned by the wall where they would jump. And the third waited near the hanging sack. All three kids touched the wall behind them.

"Get ready," Tarik said. "And . . . go!"

Meilin pushed off and ran as fast as she could. In her mind, she asked Jhi for greater speed, feeling somewhat ridiculous. It was hard to imagine extra speed coming from the sluggish panda. With swift spirit animals, Conor and Rollan had more cause for faith.

Meilin ran well, but as she approached the wall for the jump, Rollan was a few paces ahead, and Conor was about even with her. The dash felt like nothing beyond a regular sprint.

Meilin considered the jump. If the boys tried to leap high, it might slow their turn. If she focused instead on turning around quickly, she might gain ground and perhaps make it first to the hanging bag. Then again, if the jump counted for a third of her score, a weak jump might guarantee last place even if she hit the bag hard.

Ahead of her, Rollan slowed a little and jumped, slapping the wall as high as he could. It was a respectable jump, but nothing extraordinary. Meilin decided to go for it.

As she leaped, Meilin felt a strange surge of energy, and kicked off the wall to increase the height of her jump. Conor sprang beside her, and although he was taller, she slapped the wall higher.

After landing she turned and ran hard. Conor was behind her now. Rollan was a good four paces ahead and going strong.

A piercing howl cut through the room. Briggan. Though Meilin tried to ignore the noise, goose bumps rose on her arm.

Conor streaked past Meilin and passed Rollan as well. He reached the bag several steps ahead of Rollan, jumped, and slammed into it with his shoulder. He rebounded roughly, spinning to the floor, and the bag only jounced a little.

Meilin realized she needed to take care how she hit the bag. It was clearly heavy. She would treat it like she was striking a wall.

Rollan threw a punch at the bag as he ran by. The bag absorbed the impact as if it were nothing. At least Conor had moved it.

Begging for energy from Jhi, Meilin left the ground and kicked with both legs. The massive bag swayed with the impact, but not a lot. She broke her fall with her hands and rose to her feet, panting.

"Are you all right, Conor?" Tarik asked.

He rose gingerly, rubbing his shoulder. "I'm okay."

"You might have warned us it was full of rocks," Rollan complained, massaging his wrist.

"Sand," Tarik clarified. "Thoughts?"

"Not much beyond their natural talents," the female Greencloak said.

"Except toward the end of Conor's run," one of the other Greencloaks pointed out.

"How did that feel?" Tarik asked.

"When Briggan howled?" Conor asked. "I don't know — it was like I had the wind at my back. I felt more aggressive. I wasn't planning to ram the sack, but it felt right." He grimaced. "Until I hit it."

The Greencloak near the jumping wall spoke up. "Meilin may have had a little boost when she jumped."

"Did you feel it, Meilin?" Tarik asked.

"Maybe a little," she replied. "To be honest, I mostly felt on my own."

"If the panda had helped, she would have gone slower," Rollan joked.

"You certainly punched like a bird," Meilin shot back. "It was hard as a feather."

"Whoa," Rollan said, raising both hands. "Better not pick on the panda."

"No squabbling," Tarik ordered. "Your relationships with your animals are individual in nature. This isn't a contest. I mainly wanted to make each of you more aware of your spirit animal and how you might learn to help one another."

Meilin fought a stab of anger. The training exercises had only emphasized the worthlessness of her relationship with Jhi. If this was all the panda had to offer, she had made a huge mistake leaving Zhong. How could she have abandoned her father and her homeland for this?

"Are we done?" Conor asked.

Tarik exchanged nods with the other Greencloaks. "We've seen enough for now."

"What does it look like when you hit the bag?" Rollan challenged.

Tarik glanced at the other Greencloaks, then at the kids. "You'd like a demonstration?"

Meilin sighed softly. The last thing she wanted after her lackluster showing was to watch an expert in action. But the boys encouraged him.

With a flash, a sleek otter appeared.

Rollan choked back a laugh. "Your spirit animal is an otter?"

"Lumeo is more clown than beast," Tarik explained.

The otter rolled into a series of acrobatics, its long body twisting and twirling like the tail of a kite. Conor clapped.

"All right," Tarik told his beast indulgently. "We all know you're the biggest showoff here. Do you mind lending me some help for a moment?"

The otter jolted upright to attention and then watched as Tarik walked to the wall where the others had started their race. Meilin gasped when he started running. Nobody could accelerate so quickly! When he reached the wall, he kicked against it three times, gaining altitude with each step, before slapping a spot more than twice as high as anyone else had reached. As he fell, Tarik pushed off from the wall, did a backflip, and landed running. When he reached the hanging bag, his punch made it leap and quake. Then he turned away from the swinging bag.

"Amazing!" Conor said.

Rollan clapped as well, and gave a whistle.

Meilin decided she had better offer some applause or she would look like a poor sport. The display really had been quite impressive. She would never have guessed that the tall warrior could move with such speed and agility.

Tarik extended a hand to his otter. "Lumeo deserves the accolades. Without him, I could not have done any of that. We're a team, just as you are with your animals. Explore that connection, and you will be rewarded."

"Impressive," Meilin conceded. "But I feel like we're getting distracted. Zhong is under attack. People are dying. Who knows how many cities have fallen by now? I've come a long way in good faith, but I'm starting to wonder how my presence in Amaya is helping the war in Zhong. When will we learn what you Greencloaks want from us? I didn't cross Erdas to run races and kick sacks of sand."

"Soon," Tarik promised. "Olvan is finalizing his plans. You three have no idea how vital you are. We have to use you correctly. And you must try your best to be ready."

Tarik and the other Greencloaks departed. Meilin avoided further conversation with Conor and Rollan by heading directly to Jhi, who had rolled over onto her back, legs splayed out ridiculously.

"Let's go back to our room," she told the panda.

Jhi looked up expectantly.

Meilin raised her hand. "You want a lift? Guess what? As a reward for all your help, you get to walk today."

Meilin started toward her room, not caring whether the panda followed or not.

THE ISLAND

BY THE GLOW OF A LARGE YELLOW MOON, ABEKE CREPT along the rooftop behind Uraza, breathing softly. From her high vantage, she could see the lagoon where their ship had docked. The warm, humid air carried the rich smell of jungle foliage, mingled with the salty tang of the sea.

According to Shane, they were on an island in the Gulf of Amaya, on the far side of the ocean from Nilo. She had secretly explored part of it on two previous outings, confirming that it was at least a peninsula. Since she had been asleep when the ship made port, tonight she would see for herself that she was truly on an island. Not that she doubted Shane – it just gave her something to do. She had never been on an island before.

Uraza leaped down from the roof to the top of a wall. It was not a serious drop, but the landing was barely three handspans wide. As Abeke paused, Uraza looked back at her, eyes gleaming in the moonlight. Abeke felt a steadying surge of ability. The tension departed from her muscles, leaving her relaxed and limber. Her balance steadied, and she concentrated on the night sounds of the island—creatures scurrying, the call of a bird, and a hushed conversation below, perhaps on a balcony, perhaps on the ground. Her vision sharpened in the low light, and she breathed the layered scents in the air.

Abeke landed lightly on the wall, then hurried to where it joined the outer wall of the complex. After climbing a little, she dangled from the wall and dropped to the sandy ground.

Nobody had seen her escape—not that it mattered. If she got caught, the only penalty would be the sting of failure. She was hungry for practice. Her training with Shane was useful but artificial. These nighttime excursions with Uraza felt much more authentic.

Abeke followed Uraza into a ferny shadow world of tall trees with enormous leaves. She was not used to such lush vegetation, to vines and creepers, or to so many trees crowded together, but supposed the wetness in the air explained why plants thrived here. Since her arrival, it had already rained twice—short, hard downfalls that came on with little warning and ended just as swiftly. Abeke wished that she could send some of the abundant water to her village.

The stronghold where they were staying disappeared behind them. Situated just inland from the sheltered inlet where the whale-towed ships were anchored, the walled outpost contained the only buildings she had found on the island.

"Uraza, this way," Abeke said, pointing. The leopard had been veering toward the highlands they had already explored. "I want to see the far side of the island."

The big cat moved off in the desired direction. The rustling of shrubs and the cries of birds did little to disturb Abeke. She would never have ventured into this jungle alone at night, but with Uraza at her side, she felt invincible.

They prowled unhurriedly, whispering through the foliage like ghosts. Falling into an almost trancelike state, Abeke mimicked Uraza, pausing when she paused, advancing when she advanced. Through their bond, Abeke studied the leopard's techniques while borrowing her sharper senses and innate stealth.

After some time, they emerged from the trees to climb a long slope that grew steeper as they followed it. The bushes were smaller here, affording Abeke a long view of the dark forest behind her, the lights of the little outpost reduced to orange sparks near the lagoon.

From the bare ridgetop, Abeke got her first view of the farthest side of the island. The opposite slope descended sharply to the sea. By the moonlight, she could discern the coastline, partly shielded from the open water by long sandbars. There was no other land in sight. Her eyes were drawn to a pale beach in a certain cove, due to the presence of two bonfires. To blaze so brightly at this distance, the fires had to be an impressive size. Figures moved on the beach, dark specks occasionally illuminated by the firelight.

"Look down there," Abeke said. "Who could that be?"

Crouching low, Uraza watched warily beside her.

Abeke squinted, straining her sight. "Hard to tell from up here. They're a long way from the outpost. Could it be pirates? Shane said all ships have to watch out for pirates lately."

Uraza remained still beside her.

Abeke wondered if Shane's people knew they were sharing the island. Could the figures on the beach pose a threat? It seemed unlikely. There were dozens of people at the sturdy outpost, many of them armed soldiers and most with spirit animals. Three big ships waited in the lagoon. Shane had mentioned others coming soon, distinguished visitors. Could it be them on the beach? Wouldn't visitors come directly to the outpost?

"I don't like this," Abeke murmured. "I don't want to risk anybody sneaking up on Shane and his people. Think we could get close without being spotted?"

In reply, Uraza flicked her tail and started down the slope toward the cove. Abeke followed.

Soon they passed beneath trees again. Abeke took extra care to move silently. This was no longer a game. The people on the beach could be dangerous.

A balmy breeze ruffled the surrounding leaves, bringing the faint smell of smoke. Abeke welcomed the breeze – it would further disguise any sounds they made.

After a considerable hike, the smoke grew stronger and Abeke could hear distant conversations. Then, from up ahead, a shriek pierced the night. A second shriek came, less strident, followed by a third. Abeke held her breath, kneeling down beside Uraza. The cries stopped. The shrieks had not sounded human, nor did they match any animal she could think of, but they had sounded desperate.

Uraza started forward again. They advanced more

cautiously than ever, a little at a time, finally coming within sight of the beach. Together, Abeke and Uraza crept as close as they dared, gazing out from the last of the dense foliage beneath the shadows of the trees.

The twin bonfires burned wide and tall, like small huts accidentally set ablaze. By the rippling light, Abeke saw six large cages, and perhaps ten men. Four of the cages contained monstrous beasts: one was feathery, some gargantuan bird of prey; another had quills like a porcupine but was nearly the size of a buffalo; a third held a huge coiled snake, probably some kind of constrictor; and the fourth housed what appeared to be a muscular rat big enough to bring down an antelope.

An ordinary dog paced inside one of the other cages, looking small and scared compared to the neighboring monstrosities. The sixth cage stood empty.

A man in a hooded cloak approached the empty cage with a rat in his hand. The rodent was big, but nothing like the unnatural rat nearby. "Let's double the amount on this one and check for differences," he said.

"Large or small, a dose is a dose," a bald man protested.

"We have plenty," the hooded man countered. "We lost the parrot, so we have an extra cage. Let's find out firsthand."

Abeke had to strain, but she felt sure that she heard the words correctly. The hooded man produced a waterskin and upended it over the mouth of the rat in his other hand. The rat squirmed, tail whipping from side to side.

"That's enough," one of the other men growled.

"Cage it," another man demanded.

"Not yet," the hooded man said, capping the waterskin.

"If I'm too hasty, it will run out between the bars." He held out the rat for the other men to see. It wriggled in his grasp, seeming to swell. It began squirming harder, screeching in pain.

The hooded man turned and stuffed the rat between the bars of the empty cage. The rodent writhed on the cage floor, new flesh bursting out beneath its fur. It let out a tortured shriek that Abeke recognized. It squealed one more time, then lunged against the bars, its enlarged body bloated with muscle. The rat tested the bars several times, rocking the cage and kicking up sand before settling down.

Abeke could hardly trust her eyes. What would Shane think when she told him about this? Would he believe her? She glanced over at Uraza. "You're my only witness," she whispered. "You see this, don't you? It isn't natural. What did they give it?"

Uraza only looked her way for an instant, then returned her attention to the beach.

"What did I tell you?" the bald man said. "A dose is a dose. The amount don't matter."

"This one is a little larger," the hooded man said. "And if you ask me, the transformation took less time."

"Waste of effort. Let's finish this."

"This last one should be simplest," the hooded man said. "Admiral is well-trained. He may even remain so after the Bile."

"I'll believe it when I see it," the bald man said.

The hooded man held up his waterskin. "Get ready to eat your words." He walked over to the cage with the dog inside. "Sit, Admiral."

The dog sat.

"Speak."

The dog barked and wagged its tail.

The hooded man uncapped the waterskin and held it between the bars. "Come."

The dog came forward and the man poured fluid into its mouth. Abeke could see some splashing free. Then he backed away.

Several other men stepped closer to the cage, warily clutching long spears. One held a bow with an arrow set to the string.

Abeke didn't want to watch, but couldn't tear her eyes away from the sight of the dog convulsing and enlarging. It didn't cry out like the rat, but it whined softly. As the dog changed, its muscles pulled taut, bulging grotesquely. Its eyes grew fierce and wide, and foam began frothing from the corners of its mouth. The dog let out a low growl before launching itself against the side of the cage, very nearly toppling it over onto its side.

"Sit, Admiral," the hooded man called from a distance.

The monstrous dog shifted into a sitting position.

"Speak."

The beefy dog let out a powerful bark that resonated through the jungle, sending birds flying from the trees.

"Good boy, Admiral," the hooded man called. "Good boy."

"All right, I'm impressed," the bald man admitted. "But I wouldn't let it out without a leash."

Some of the other men chuckled. Most still held their weapons cautiously.

A swirling breeze stirred the air.

Suddenly the dog whipped its head toward the jungle, staring directly at Abeke. It let out a rumbling growl. Some of the men glanced in the direction the dog was staring. Abeke resisted the urge to immediately retreat. If she moved while their eyes were on her, she would give herself away for sure. She had to rely on the leaves and the shadows.

The dog's growl built into a series of vicious barks.

"What is it, Admiral?" the hooded man called, following the animal's gaze.

The huge dog barked more fiercely.

"No, no, no," Abeke whispered.

The dog began to savagely ram the sides of the cage. The men were shouting to each other, but Abeke couldn't make out their words under the noise. Barking and thrashing, the dog went into a frenzy. The cage shuddered violently. The dog began bashing the roof, and the wood began to crack and splinter.

Abeke felt sharp teeth on her arm. Uraza was gently biting her. Once Abeke noticed her, the leopard slunk back deeper into the trees. Abeke joined her retreat.

The wild clamor continued behind her, and then there was a violent crack. Glancing over her shoulder, Abeke saw the enormous hound crash through the roof of the cage, the bars falling away in all directions. Ignoring the men, some of whom made halfhearted jabs with their spears, the monstrous dog raced straight toward Abeke, spewing sand with each massive stride.

Uraza broke into a run with Abeke sprinting beside her. All pretense at stealth abandoned, Abeke tore through the jungle, wishing she had brought more weaponry than a knife. Then again, what good would any weapon do against the savage dog?

The animal stampeded behind them. Ferocious barks and growls impelled Abeke forward. There was no time to strategize—she ran with everything she had, driven by pure terror. The same terrain that had permitted her to creep alongside Uraza now tripped her up. Branches lashed her body, roots grabbed her ankles, and the uneven ground was treacherous. She stumbled to her knees several times and fell flat once, but always rose as quickly as she could, clawing at the vegetation, half running, half swimming through the leaves.

The gigantic dog was gaining rapidly. Any moment, those teeth would seize her. She had lost sight of Uraza. The dog was nearly upon her. Determined not to be an easy victim, Abeke drew her knife and whirled.

Her senses abruptly sharpened. She saw the overgrown canine coming and shrank into a comfortable crouch. As it lunged, she sprang sideways, swinging her knife. The tip of the blade scratched the brute's flank as the beast blurred past her.

Abeke put a tree between herself and the dog. It struck the tree with enough force to shake the jungle, but the trunk held. Abeke raced away, but the frothing dog pursued her relentlessly. She tripped, rolled onto her back, and held up her knife in desperation. The dog surged forward, mouth gaping, teeth huge in the darkness.

With a screaming roar unlike any cry Abeke had ever heard, Uraza hurtled out of the night, her jaws closing on the side of the dog's neck. The impact broke the dog's rushing attack. Leopard and dog tumbled together in the darkness, narrowly missing Abeke, snarling and spitting, teeth flashing, claws slashing.

Abeke's first instinct was to run. Her second thought was to help Uraza. But then she got the distinct impression that she should climb. The notion came so strongly that she leaped to the nearest tree, embracing the trunk with arms and knees. There were no branches to grip, but she pulled with her arms and clamped with her knees, somehow heaving herself higher and higher.

At last she found short limbs where she could rest. Behind her, she saw Uraza had taken to a tree as well, a red wound marring her magnificent pelt. Below, the frustrated dog barked and bayed and finally howled. Abeke's tree shook as the dog rammed it with manic tenacity. She held tight. She had lost her knife. Her only hope was to outlast her attacker.

Something caught the dog's attention and it ran over to another tree. Dimly, in the leaf-filtered moonlight, Abeke saw a figure high in the branches. It held a bow, and was launching arrow after arrow down at the dog.

The huge dog leaped and barked and growled. It clawed futilely at the trunk. No matter how many arrows found their mark, it didn't seek cover. Finally, with a slow inevitability, the arrows did their job. The creature sank back, took two wobbly steps, then collapsed on the forest floor with a plaintive whine.

The figure climbed down from the tree. He paused beside the rapidly shrinking dog, then came to the base of Abeke's tree. "Come down, Abeke," a hushed voice called. She knew the voice. "It's dead. Come down – we need to go."

Hugging the trunk, Abeke shinnied down the tree and dropped to the ground. "Shane! How did you find me?"

"Did you think I'd let you roam the jungle alone at night?" he replied.

"You followed me?"

"Not so loud," Shane warned, looking away through the trees. "I'd rather the men on the beach not find us."

"The men," Abeke said, lowering her voice. "They made the dog into a monster! They fed it something."

"I know about them," Shane said. "I didn't know they were here tonight until it was too late. Otherwise I would have steered you away."

"How far back were you?"

"Too far. I try not to make my presence known, although I'm sure I never fooled your leopard."

"What were those men doing?"

"They're trying to find a replacement for the Nectar. They try out their concoctions in secret."

"The Nectar doesn't create monsters!"

"These men are testing different substances," Shane said. "I don't know all their goals. It would not end well if they caught us. We should go."

Uraza prowled into view, her side bleeding. Crouching beside her leopard, Abeke flung her arms around her neck. "Thank you," Abeke murmured. "You saved my life."

VISION

IN A LOFTY ANTECHAMBER, DAYLIGHT STREAMED THROUGH A stained-glass window, splashing colorful patterns across the floor. Briggan explored the area, sniffing the corners and the furniture. When the wolf passed through the tinted light, dappled hues glossed his gray-white coat. Conor had lost track of how long they had waited. It frustrated him that even though he was no longer a servant to Devin, he was still stuck inside a castle all the time. He could tell that Briggan didn't love being cooped up either.

The door opened and Rollan emerged with Essix on his shoulder. Conor and Briggan looked up expectantly. Apparently Lenori and Rollan were finally done.

"Your turn," Rollan said.

"How was it?" Conor asked.

Rollan shrugged. "She wanted to know about my dreams. If it was a test, I don't think I passed. Have fun."

Conor entered the room where Lenori waited in a large, padded chair that dwarfed her petite frame. Her green cloak rested on a nearby table. Feathers were braided into her long hair and several beaded necklaces and bracelets hung from her neck and wrists. Her bare feet rested on a low ottoman, her soles callused and brown.

Beside her chair, a peculiar bird roosted on a tall, portable perch. The bird had a slender neck, a down-curved bill, and vibrant plumage of every shade. Lenori indicated a nearby chair to Conor. He sat down, Briggan on the floor near him. She looked at him with eyes as unfathomable as the ocean. He wondered if she could read his mind.

"How are you, Conor?"

The question was posed mildly, and seemed sincere. "Me? Honestly? I keep wondering whether Briggan came to the right person."

Lenori smiled. "No beast would bond with the wrong person, least of all a Great Beast. Where does this worry come from?"

Conor regretted having expressed the concern. Her posture was relaxed, but there was no escaping those watchful eyes. "All of this is just so far beyond anything I ever expected."

"I think I understand." Her voice was gentle and melodious. "Don't pressure yourself to evolve overnight. You'll grow into this role. Tell me about your dreams since Briggan arrived."

Conor considered the question. "Once, in real life, I had to fight off a pack of wolves from the sheep I protected. I've had to relive that night in my dreams a lot lately." He glanced over at Briggan, who had his mouth open with his tongue hanging out. It was the closest a wolf could get to smiling.

"Have any other animals visited your dreams?" Lenori asked.

"I don't know," Conor said. "I saw a ram not long ago. The kind with big curly horns."

Lenori leaned forward. "Where was it? What was it doing?"

The circumstances returned to him vividly. It had been the rare sort of dream that felt exactly like real life, even in memory. He had been climbing a high, rugged mountain, the rough stone as cold as ice beneath his palms. Scaling a sheer face, he had reached a point where he could progress no farther, nor could he descend the way he had come.

As the wind kicked up, he had clung to the mountainside miserably, knowing he could continue or retreat, and either way he would fall. His muscles burning, the air too thin to satisfy his lungs, he had held on as tight as he could, knowing that eventually his strength would fail and he would plummet to the base of the cliff. Why had he climbed so high?

Since holding still meant certain death, he'd decided that he had to keep going, no matter how scant the handholds. Stretching, he hooked his fingertips over a tiny wrinkle in the rock overhead. As he searched for his next handhold, the sun crested the mountaintop, blinding him.

Squinting, grimacing, arms burning, toes slipping, he fumbled for anything to grab with his right hand. Then a shadow had fallen across him, and he peered up at the huge silhouette of a ram, staring down at him from higher still up the cliff. The sight of the beast had made him forget his peril. He had stared for a long moment before his hands failed him. He gave an agonized scream and then he fell, his stomach lurching to his throat as he hurtled toward the ground. Just as he was about to hit, he woke up, slick with sweat.

"I was in the mountains," Conor said. "I saw it right before I woke up. The sun was in my eyes. The ram was big, but it was hard to see details."

"Have you ever worked with bighorn sheep?" Lenori asked.

"No. But I've seen pictures of Arax. My parents have one. The ram in my dreams was like him."

"Was it like him, or was it him?"

Conor was very conscious of her heightened interest. Didn't she ever blink? He knew the answer, but felt awkward. He worried it would come across like he was trying to sound important. He glanced away, then back. "It was just a dream. But, yeah, I think it was Arax."

"Have you dreamed about any of the other Great Beasts? Rumfuss? Tellun? Do you know all of them?"

Conor chuckled uncomfortably. "I know there are fifteen, the Four Fallen plus the other eleven. I'm no expert. I can name some of them—Cabaro the Lion, Mulop the Octopus. Arax, of course. Shepherds pay extra attention to him. With enough time I could maybe remember them all."

"The Great Beasts have protected Erdas since time out of mind. We would all do better to be more familiar with them. Besides the four obvious ones and those you named, we have Tellun the Elk, Ninani the Swan, Halawir the Eagle, Dinesh the Elephant, Rumfuss the Boar, Suka the Polar Bear, Kovo the Ape, and Gerathon the Serpent."

Conor noticed Briggan's ears prick up. "I haven't

dreamed about the others. Just that ram. Do you mind me asking why you're so interested?"

"I doubt it was an ordinary dream."

Briggan stood up, watching her intently.

"The wolf seems to agree," Lenori said.

Briggan barked, making Conor jump.

"Dreams can range from the meaningless to the prophetic," Lenori said. "It usually takes experience to discern one from the other. The dreams Rollan and Meilin shared with me were of little consequence. I hoped for more from Meilin, but she needs to grow closer to Jhi first. I suspected your dreams might be weightier, and you haven't disappointed me."

Conor shifted in his chair. "Why'd you suspect me?"

"Briggan was among the more visionary of the Great Beasts. He is known by the titles Packleader, Moonrunner, and, significantly, Pathfinder."

Conor reached out and rubbed the coarse mane on the back of Briggan's neck. "Are you really all of those things?"

Briggan turned his head, his tongue lolling out in another wolfish grin.

"I too have seen Arax the Ram lately," Lenori said. "That is why we gathered at the Sunset Tower in Amaya, the nearest Greencloak tower to his current domain."

"You know where to find him?" Conor asked.

"I don't know his exact location," Lenori said. "But I hope we may be able to find him together. Aside from the recent return of Briggan and the Fallen, none have encountered the Great Beasts for many years. Arax is among the most solitary. He prefers the mountaintops, exercising his influence over the winds and terrain in the highest places of the world. We can't trust luck or woodcraft to find him. The wilds of western Amaya are untamed. Unguided, we could search for years and never get close."

Lenori paused for a moment, then spoke in a softer voice. "Would you mind trying for a waking vision?"

"Me?" Conor asked. He was no prophet. "What do you mean?"

"Briggan may be able to use your connection to share information glimpsed from afar."

Conor rubbed his hands over his eyes. "I wouldn't know how to begin."

Lenori crossed to Conor and knelt before him. She took both of his hands in hers. He tried not to go completely rigid.

"Unbeknownst to some Greencloaks," Lenori explained, "spirit animals do not only exist to let us swing a sword harder. There can be aspects to the connection more valuable than running fast or jumping high. If you relax, I believe I can show you."

"I'll try if you want," Conor said. He certainly couldn't relax with her holding his hands.

Perhaps sensing this, Lenori backed away. "Don't try to force it," she instructed. "Relax and gaze upon Myriam, my rainbow ibis. Watch her as you would a campfire on a lonely night."

The bird on the perch spread her multicolored wings. She bobbed gently, causing cascades of color to ripple through her vivid feathers. Trying to follow Lenori's instructions, Conor thought about how he watched campfires. He tried not to stare hard at a fixed point. Without searching for anything specific, he let the rainbow ibis serve as his center of attention.

Lenori was speaking but Conor got lost in the cadence of her words. Her voice was rhythmic, a melodic pulse that steadied and calmed him. Dimly he noticed Briggan turning in a circle, first one way, then the other. He began to feel very drowsy. He blinked his eyes, but it didn't seem to help. In fact, with every blink, the room became more of a blur.

Conor stared down a misty tunnel. Where had that come from? He soared down the hazy passage without any sensation of movement. At its end, he saw a grizzly-bear and a raccoon hurrying across a wide brown prairie. With an effort of will, he sped up until he glided along-side them.

There was no wind in his face, no physical evidence of his speed. But the shaggy grizzly bear ran hard, as did the raccoon. Both kept their eyes fixed on the hori-zon. Looking ahead, Conor saw a spectacular mountain range. Atop a distant ridge, the great ram was outlined in sunlight.

As soon as his eyes locked on the ram, Conor found himself pulled from behind. Against his will, he with-drew back into the misty tunnel until the animals became specks in the distance. The tunnel collapsed and dissolved. Conor realized that Lenori, Briggan, and the rainbow ibis were all staring at him. He felt clammy. His mouth tasted weird and oddly fuzzy, like after a long sleep.

"What did you see?" Lenori inquired serenely.

"Huh?" He felt unsteady. "I . . . I saw a raccoon and a big, shaggy bear. They were running toward some mountains. I could see Arax beyond them, up high on the rocks. They were heading straight at him."

"A bear and a raccoon," Lenori repeated. "Anything else?"

"I didn't notice much else. I was mostly focused on the bear and the raccoon. I had to go through a long tunnel."

Lenori gave a triumphant smile. She took his hand, squeezing it gently. "You did it, Conor. I think you found our path."

In less than an hour, Conor was escorted past a dozen armed guards and through multiple sets of double doors to a high room with the curtains drawn. He found Olvan, Lenori, Tarik, Rollan, and Meilin waiting, along with all of their spirit animals. Tarik's otter darted around the room in bursts of motion, clambering across furniture and bookcases. Tarik's pairing with Lumeo seemed odd, since the tall Greencloak was so serious. Olvan's moose stood near the fireplace, its massive form out of place indoors. The dignified room had a feel similar to the Earl of Trunswick's study, but it was even bigger.

Olvan stood up, rubbed his big hands together, and swept the room with his keen, knowing gaze. In spite of the white in his hair and beard, he had thick, powerful limbs and a broad chest. Age had not yet robbed him of strength or vigor. Conor could easily imagine him astride his moose, leading an army into battle.

The commander of the Greencloaks noisily cleared his throat. "I know we have kept you in suspense regarding the roles we hope you will play. You can blame me for the delay—I prefer to know the whole story before I share it. Joining the Greencloaks is merely the first step toward the vital purpose we hope you'll serve. Given recent developments"—he nodded toward Conor—"the time to act is upon us."

Olvan strolled over to the mantel. When he turned to face the others, his expression was grave. "Centuries and centuries ago, in the last worldwide war, the four nations of Erdas battled the Devourer and his army of Conquerors. Two Great Beasts aided the Devourer—Kovo the Ape and Gerathon the Serpent. Four of the Great Beasts sided with us. Three of them are here today."

Olvan paused to let that sink in. Feeling unworthy, Conor considered Briggan. The wolf sat listening attentively.

"Before the original Essix, Briggan, Jhi, and Uraza joined the fight, we were losing the war. None of the continents went unscathed. Most of Nilo and Zhong had fallen. The Zhongese and Niloans who escaped fled to Eura and Amaya, only to find those nations besieged as well. Cities were razed. Food was in short supply. It was only a matter of time before the Devourer declared victory.

"The Greencloaks were a fledgling organization then, but when four of the Great Beasts showed their support, the Marked flocked to join us. The Greencloaks did what nobody else had done—they mounted a major offensive, taking the fight to the Devourer. The four Great Beasts gave their lives in the fight, which is why they are known as the Four Fallen. But the Devourer fell as well, and Kovo and Gerathon were captured. The cost was great, but the four nations emerged victorious and began to rebuild."

"What about the rest of the beasts?" Rollan asked. "The other nine?"

Olvan shrugged. "Seeing the damage that two of their own had caused, a few of the Great Beasts offered their aid at the very end. Tellun the Elk, the most powerful of them all, imprisoned Kovo and Gerathon for their crimes, and Ninani the Swan gifted the Greencloaks with the secret to creating Nectar. The rest . . . well, the Great Beasts are a strange group. They are seldom unanimous on any issue, and their purposes are almost inscrutable. They tend to remain aloof, only getting involved during times of the direst peril."

"The Devourer didn't count as serious trouble?" Rollan scoffed.

Olvan sighed. "One can only speculate. Perhaps some of the Great Beasts felt it best to protect their own territory, or their talismans."

Conor looked at Lenori, a question in his eyes.

"Each of the Great Beasts protects a unique talisman," Lenori inserted. "A totem that houses great power."

"Except for Kovo, Gerathon, and the Fallen Beasts," Meilin said. "Their talismans vanished after the war. Some suspect that Tellun asked Halawir the Eagle to hide them."

"Very good," Olvan said. "You've studied your history. The events surrounding the Great Beasts are often dismissed as legend. I am glad that some in Zhong have considered those deeds worth remembering outside of children's tales."

Meilin reddened slightly. "I heard about that from my nanny, not my instructors."

Olvan frowned. "The Great Beasts have been out of sight for a long time. We honor the Fallen on our flags, we paint pictures, we build statues, we tell stories, but for most people, the Great Beasts belong to a time long past. Some doubt whether they ever even existed."

"I was one of those," Rollan said. "Until Essix came along."

Olvan nodded. "You're not to be blamed. It's a prevalent opinion, shared in varying measures by the Prime Minister of Amaya, the Queen of Eura, the Emperor of Zhong, and the High Chieftain of Nilo. And yet, during the most critical crossroads in history, the Great Beasts have always played a major role. We are now rushing toward a crisis where the Great Beasts may prove more important than ever."

"You think the Devourer is back?" Meilin asked, her whole body quivering with agitation. "You think that is who attacked Zhong? Why weren't we warned?"

"We had only our suspicions," Olvan said sadly. "My voice has been raised in warning to the leaders of all the nations. But I cannot force them to heed me."

"And we still don't know the whole story," Lenori explained.

Olvan nodded. "We get new information every day. Whether we're up against the same Devourer who leveled much of Erdas long ago, or some inheritor of his legacy, we're still not sure. What is sure is this—the Devourer can raise vast, powerful armies in a short time. He can be patient and subtle, or ruthless and brash, depending on the need. He inspires manic devotion in his followers.

And he would gladly destroy the civilized world to rule over its ashes."

"What do we need to do?" Conor asked.

Olvan glanced at Conor, Meilin, and Rollan in turn. "Our spies have learned that the Devourer has once again made collecting the talismans a top priority. Each talisman has different powers that can be used by one of the Marked. Our enemy wishes to employ those powers against us. So we're going to recover the talismans before he can."

"Wait," Rollan said as the color drained from his face. "You want *us* to go after the talismans of the Great Beasts?"

"You won't go alone," Olvan said. "The Greencloaks have no finer warrior than Tarik. He will serve as your guide and protector. I lament that you're all so young, but your connections to the Fallen will be critical in finding and retrieving the talismans. These talismans could change the course of the war. All of Erdas needs you."

As the full enormity of the task hit him, Conor felt light-headed. How was he supposed to go up against a Great Beast? This was beyond dangerous. Olvan had basically handed them a death sentence.

He reached out a hand to Briggan. The wolf nuzzled his palm. Without Briggan, they wouldn't know where to find Arax. Conor tried to steel himself. Olvan was right: If the Devourer wanted these talismans, the Greencloaks had to get to them first. Conor wasn't sure how they would, but they needed to try. "We'll do our part," Conor pledged, though his voice broke on the words.

"Speak for yourself," Rollan said.

"I meant me and Briggan," Conor explained, flushing.

"Oh, right," Rollan replied. He faced Olvan. "Well, I see why you need us. My question is what do we get out of it? Besides risking our lives to do something we're not ready for."

"As a Greencloak, this is your duty," Lenori said calmly. "Your reward would be the same as ours—the satisfaction of defending what is right, defending Erdas."

"I'm not a Greencloak," Rollan said. "I may never join."

"We'll do it," Meilin said, giving Rollan a disgusted glance. "Jhi and I. This is what I hoped for—a chance to make a difference. I've seen what's coming. Zhong has the best armies in the world, and these new Conquerors are tearing us apart. We mustn't let them get more power. They must be stopped. It would be my honor to join your ranks and defend Zhong as you describe."

Conor studied Meilin with admiration and a little bit of fear. He could scarcely imagine what hardships awaited, but at least he and Briggan wouldn't face them alone. Who did Rollan think he was? What reward did he expect?

Rollan sighed. "And if I don't want to become a Greencloak?"

"How selfish can you *be*?" Meilin seethed. "Zhong is under attack. The rest of Erdas will be soon. What other big offers do you expect the world to give a coward during wartime?"

"I never had any offers until Essix showed up," Rollan snapped. "The Greencloaks only cared about me once I got my bird. There's a city full of orphans just like me who Olvan was all too happy to pass by until he found Essix. Maybe I wonder why the Greencloaks only include Marked people. Maybe I wonder who put them in charge of the Great Beasts and the talismans. And maybe, unlike you, I don't love getting pushed into situations I don't understand! I want to know exactly who I'm working for and why."

Olvan glanced at Tarik and Lenori. Slowly he stood and walked to where Rollan was seated, until he stood right before him, staring down. Conor wondered if he was trying to intimidate Rollan, but when the large man spoke, his voice was controlled. "I can understand wanting to take your time with a decision this big. I believe that time spent among the Greencloaks will relieve your doubts as to our sincerity. We don't believe we're in charge of the Great Beasts. We do our jobs because we know that, along with the Great Beasts, we're the last line of defense."

"What about the governments?" Rollan asked. "The prime minister and all of them."

Olvan made a skeptical face. "They do what they do. They administer. They make and enforce laws. They squabble about commerce and they occasionally fight with each other. It's just squabbling, human squabbling. But we were gifted to see something beyond the concerns of man. We were each gifted with a spirit animal. And so we will protect Erdas – all of Erdas – with everything we have."

Rollan compressed his lips. "I'm not crazy. I don't want Erdas to become a wasteland." He considered. "What – what if I'm not ready to join the Greencloaks, but I'm willing to help?"

"May I suggest another option for you?" Olvan said.

"We frequently work with Marked individuals who don't accept our vows. We don't normally give them access to our weightiest secrets, but these circumstances are extraordinary."

"Let me sleep on it," Rollan said.

Conor turned away and closed his eyes. Regardless of who else came along, tomorrow he would venture into the wilderness to chase a legend. Leaning close to his wolf, he whispered, "What have we gotten ourselves into?"

10

DREAM

MEILIN STROLLED ALONG A WOODEN WALKWAY THROUGH A manicured garden, a fragile parasol on her shoulder. She reached a bridge over a brook between two ponds. Below, ornamental carp swam in lazy circles, flashing their red, orange, yellow, and white scales among the purple blossoms of the water lilies.

Trees and shrubbery screened the house from view, but Meilin would have recognized any portion of her grandfather Xao's garden. She had grown up roaming these pathways, enveloped in the scent of these blossoms.

Up ahead, a panda was coming her way. Meilin scrunched her brow. Besides the fish in the ponds and the birds in the trees, animals had never been part of the garden.

The panda came to her on the bridge and stood up on its hind legs. "You miss Zhong," the panda said in a rich female voice. Somehow, Meilin wasn't surprised to hear it speak.

"Why should I miss it?"

The panda offered no reply.

Suddenly Meilin remembered everything. Lenori had taken her away from Zhong. While her father fought a terrible horde, Meilin had run away to the other side of the world—Amaya, the New Lands.

How had she reached this garden? She hadn't. This was a dream.

Meilin regarded the panda curiously. "Are you Jhi?"

The panda gave a nod. "I am sorry to be a disappointment to you."

"You're not . . ." Meilin began, but couldn't finish. She sighed. "We're at war. I'd hoped for an animal that could help me fight. I like you, but . . . my home, and my father, are in danger."

"I want to like you too. Give me a chance and you may find I'm more useful than you suppose."

"Lenori told me that you were known as a skillful healer. You were called Peacefinder and Healthbringer."

"Among other things. Meilin, heed my words. You should get inside. This is no kind of weather for a stroll."

Meilin peered up at the sky. The only clouds were distant, wispy, and white. The sun glared brightly. "It doesn't look bad."

"You don't want to be here," the panda said.

The warning made her uncertain, and she felt a faint chill. Meilin looked around for danger.

"Close your eyes," Jhi insisted. "Ignore this illusion. Pay careful attention."

Meilin closed her eyes. Pay attention to what? A frosty sensation chilled her skin. Yes, now that she noticed, she felt very cold. And wet. She hugged herself, shivering.

Meilin opened her eyes, but the garden was unchanged. The panda stared at her.

"I'm cold," Meilin said.

"You don't want to be here," Jhi repeated.

Meilin turned and ran along the wooden walkway. The day remained pleasant around her, but her skin felt cold and wet. Thumping down the wooden walkway, she followed the turns that would lead to the door in the wall. Maybe if she could escape the garden, she could escape the dream.

The door came into view. Unsettled by the strange chill, Meilin kept watching for danger, but the garden remained tranquil. When she reached the door, she found it locked. She jiggled the handle and leaned her shoulder against it, but the door refused to budge.

Meilin paused. Goose bumps pimpled her arms. This was a dream. What if she imagined herself stronger than the door? Backing up a few steps, she lowered her shoulder and charged.

The impact felt jarringly real. As she stumbled back and fell to the ground, Meilin jolted awake, her eyes opening to a confusing scene. It was dark. Rain poured down on her soaked nightclothes. By the muted moonlight, Meilin could make out that she was on the roof of a tower bordered by battlements. This was Sunset Tower! But what was she doing up here in the middle of the night during a rainstorm?

Freezing and completely drenched, Meilin shakily arose.

Before her stood a sturdy wooden door, slick from the

rainfall. She tried the handle. It was locked. Her shoulder still ached from ramming it.

This was the third time she had sleepwalked since summoning Jhi. There had never been a dream associated with the experience, but twice before she had woken up doing odd things in unusual places. This, however, was the strangest by far.

Meilin tried the door again. It held fast. Would anyone hear her if she yelled? If she banged long enough?

Meilin had told Lenori about the sleepwalking. The Amayan had explained that people adapted to new bonds in all sorts of bizarre ways. Vivid nightmares were common. Mood swings. Panic attacks. Even rashes. All sorts of side effects had been observed. Developing a pattern of sleepwalking was not terribly strange.

But this was ridiculous! Her teeth were chattering. She was in real danger from the cold.

Meilin banged on the door and yelled, but her efforts didn't make much noise. The wind picked up, making her so cold that she whimpered. She stomped in place and flapped her arms, trying to generate warmth.

Then she heard the latch unfasten, and the door opened.

There was no light beyond the door. "Hello?" Meilin called softly, hands balled into fists, hesitant to cross into the deeper darkness. The cold, stinging raindrops continued their assault.

A flash of lightning, the first since she had awoken, briefly illuminated a black-and-white form.

"Jhi?" Meilin asked. Thunder boomed. The doorway was dark again. "Is that you?"

The panda gave no reply. Meilin felt stupid for expecting one.

Meilin stepped out of the rain, closed the door, then knelt down and hugged the panda. Jhi felt warm and perfect. Meilin embraced her for a long time, sinking into her thick fur and enjoying her scent as never before.

"I was sleepwalking again," Meilin whispered. "I got myself into real trouble this time. Thanks for finding me."

The panda didn't respond, but Meilin felt like she understood. Meilin stood up, placing a hand against the nearest wall to help her feel her way in the dark. "Let's get back to bed."

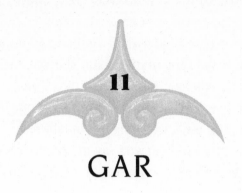

GAR

"ABEKE!" SHANE CALLED. "ABEKE, WHERE ARE YOU?"

Abeke kept still in her tree, a slow smile parting her lips. Uraza crouched motionless on a limb beside her.

Down below, Shane blundered closer to her hiding place. "This is the wrong time for games! Remember those important people I told you about? They're here! We shouldn't keep them waiting."

Ever since their ship had reached this island, Shane had gone on and on about these visitors. He seemed very impressed by them.

In many ways, Shane was her first real friend. Not only had he saved her life, but he continued to train with her, watch out for her, and even joke with her. He appreciated her hunting, her strength, her stealth—many of the traits that she most valued. Only her mother had ever made her feel accepted in that way.

Yet she had questions about the people he worked with. None wore green cloaks, but they seemed well organized. They had ships, a big outpost, and many trained soldiers.

All had spirit animals. Who were they, and why did they leave Uraza so agitated? Lately, she hadn't pressed Shane for answers. She was afraid of what she might learn.

But that wasn't the main reason she was hiding.

"All right, Abeke," Shane said. "I admit it. You keep improving. Even on this puny island, you and Uraza could probably evade me for as long as you chose."

"I just wanted to hear you say it," Abeke replied.

"There you are!" Shane greeted. "You picked the worst time to prove a point."

Abeke descended from the tree. Uraza landed beside her. "You backed down, so I must have chosen the right time."

"You and Uraza are really coming along as a team," Shane said. "Our visitors will be pleased."

"They're really here?" Abeke asked. He might have simply been trying to lure her out of hiding.

"They're not just here," Shane said. "They're waiting for us."

She felt nervous, but hoped it didn't show. "Lead the way."

They started walking toward the walled buildings. "You should probably put Uraza into her dormant state."

"Won't they want to see her?" Abeke asked.

"It proves your abilities," Shane said. "You're young to use the dormant state. It also shows respect. Some of their spirit animals don't get along well with others. If you keep Uraza with you, they'll have to make their animals passive. It would be rude."

Abeke could see what he meant, but wasn't it rude for them to expect her to put Uraza away if their animals were the unfriendly ones? The visitors clearly meant a lot to Shane, so she decided not to argue. Abeke held out her arm and called to Uraza. With a stinging flash, the leopard became a tattoo.

It was not far to the walled stronghold. They passed through a massive iron gate and Shane led Abeke to the central building. They entered and went to the main chamber. A pair of guards who Abeke didn't recognize stood outside a set of heavy doors. They bowed to Shane and let them pass.

The visitors were assembled at the far side of the large stone room. A throne had been set up, and on it sat a regal man just entering his autumn years. His temples were touched with gray, and he had a craggy face with a jutting chin. A circlet ringed his head, wrought like a snake consuming its own tail. Below his heavy eyebrows, dark eyes watched Abeke intently.

Before his throne stretched an enormous crocodile. Abeke had no idea they could grow so large. From snout to tail, it was longer than five grown men lying end to end.

"He's a king," Abeke murmured to Shane.

"Yes," Shane muttered back. "Behave accordingly."

To one side of the king crouched a wizened old woman on a stool, bundled in coarse rags. Drool dribbled from one corner of her withered lips. On the other side of the throne stood Zerif. He was dressed in fancier clothes than when they had last met, and his hair was slicked back.

"Zerif!" Abeke cried. Her eyes had been so drawn to the man on the throne and to the crocodile that she had been slow to recognize her former protector.

He gave a polite nod. "I told you that we would meet

again." He gestured toward the throne. "May I introduce General Gar, king of the Lost Lands. Sire, meet Abeke, the summoner of Uraza."

"No small feat," said the man on the throne. He had a voice that carried weight. It wasn't terribly deep but, like his face, it was full of presence. A voice accustomed to giving orders.

"Is that your crocodile?" Abeke asked.

General Gar raised his eyebrows. "Indeed. A saltwater crocodile, from the continent of Stetriol."

Abeke frowned. Stetriol? Erdas had four regions, and none were named Stetriol. She shivered as her eyes strayed to the huge reptile. Abeke had only heard of one person who ever had a saltwater crocodile as a spirit animal. The Devourer.

"What are you thinking, Abeke?" General Gar asked. "Speak freely."

"It's just that . . ." Abeke hesitated. "I've seldom heard of a big crocodile like this as a spirit animal."

"Only once, am I right?" General Gar said with a knowing grin. He waved a dismissive hand. "It gets mentioned all the time. The Devourer, from the children's stories, was said to have been paired with a saltwater crocodile. But he died long ago. I know it is rare across the rest of Erdas, but in Stetriol, summoning a saltwater crocodile is no cause for astonishment. It occurs from time to time."

Abeke looked to Shane, and then to Zerif. They seemed at ease. "I see."

"It's true, Abeke," Shane said. "The histories don't mention Stetriol, but it's a real place. I was born there."

"He's right," Zerif assured her. "The Greencloaks wrote

the histories, and they deliberately ignored Stetriol. No surprise there. They committed horrible crimes against the people of our continent."

Abeke measured up Zerif. "You told me you work with Greencloaks."

"I do, on occasion. Some of them are very good people. Others seek to dominate the world. The organization has been corrupt for a long time, and is getting worse. Listen, nobody knows more about the Devourer than the people of Stetriol—we were the first continent he conquered, all those years ago. We were grateful when the Greencloaks freed us from his evil rule, until they turned on us. Women, children—the Greencloaks tried to wipe out all life on Stetriol, as if the common people were responsible for what the Devourer had done. We had suffered under the tyranny of the Devourer, and then we suffered worse after the Greencloaks defeated him. Only by hiding did any of us survive." Zerif's dark eyes held Abeke captive. "The Greencloaks were ashamed of their actions and tried to hide the fact that Stetriol ever existed. For the most part, they succeeded. They removed it from the histories and from the maps. But not all the people in Stetriol perished. The survivors had descendants. General Gar is their king."

Abeke shot a curious glance at Shane. This information was new to her, but she supposed it was all plausible.

"You are understandably puzzled," General Gar said. "Perhaps you imagine yourself among enemies, for that is how the Greencloaks characterize everyone but themselves. Nothing could be further from the truth."

Chinwe was the only Greencloak Abeke had actually

known. She had always seemed kind of mysterious, but had genuinely cared about the village. In the stories, the Greencloaks were always the good guys, but if the Greencloaks had written the stories . . .

Shifting on his throne, General Gar raised his eyebrows. "The war happened long ago. We do not hate the Greencloaks. The butchers who slaughtered our ancestors are long gone. But you must forgive us if we are slow to trust them. They tried to exterminate us once, and we fear they may do the same again. This is why we have endured centuries without the Nectar, our people suffering the illness and death that accompanies natural bonding."

Abeke looked to Shane again. "How awful! Your bonding . . ."

"Occurred without any Nectar," Shane said. "I was one of the lucky ones. Other friends and family weren't." Abeke realized with surprise that Shane's eyes were wet. She had never seen him look so vulnerable.

"We mean the Greencloaks no harm," General Gar said. "We mean no harm to the other nations of Erdas. We just want the chance to protect our people from the side effects of natural bonding. Our problem is that the Greencloaks control all the Nectar, and use that control to wield power over the people of Erdas. The Greencloaks should make the Nectar available to everyone."

"They share it," Abeke said, thinking of Chinwe.

"The good ones do," General Gar agreed. "But they only share it on their terms. In return, they want influence, control. And those are the best of them. Some keep it for themselves. Or, worse, they share false Nectar. It is already a terrible problem in Zhong and Amaya, and the problem is spreading."

"That doesn't seem very fair," Abeke admitted.

"Exactly," Shane said. "But we can't risk asking them directly. If they know people survive in Stetriol, they might come destroy us."

"We have a plan to help them listen to reason," Zerif said. "Did you know that each of the Great Beasts possesses a talisman?"

"I think so," Abeke said, unsure. "My mother mentioned them in the stories she told."

"All of the talismans contain powers that can be used by the Marked," Zerif explained. "The Greencloaks are currently seeking the talismans of the Great Beasts. They wish to control all of the talismans just as they control the world's supply of Nectar."

"We intend to claim the talismans first," General Gar said. "That way the Greencloaks will have to listen to us. And the talismans will give us some protection in case the Greencloaks try to wipe out Stetriol again. We cannot lose more loved ones to the consequences of natural bonding. With our modest numbers, we are risking everything to obtain a few of these talismans. Abeke, we hope that you and Uraza will help us."

Abeke felt confused. "Me? How can I help? I know nothing about any talismans. Unless . . . do you think Uraza has one?"

"Uraza lost her talisman when she was killed, as did the other Four Fallen," Zerif said. "No one knows where they ended up. We have people investigating those. Shane's sister, Drina, leads that team."

"We don't require information from you," General Gar clarified, and gestured to the crone on the stool. "We have Yumaris. Her spirit animal is an earthworm. Yumaris has lost touch with daily life, but she sees with a penetrating eye. She is how Zerif found you. She recently located one of the talismans, in Amaya. I want you to join Zerif and Shane to help us retrieve it."

"You and Uraza can help repair the world," Zerif said, his face intent. "Join us in protecting our homeland and helping to make the Nectar available to all who need it."

Abeke frowned. Something didn't feel right. She trusted Shane, but it was all so much to absorb. "What about the men who were making monsters?"

General Gar nodded. "Shane informed me about your unfortunate encounter. Those were not our men, but I am aware of them. They constantly experiment in the attempt to find a replacement for the Nectar. I applaud their desire to make Nectar freely available, but I have no love for their methods."

"It was a terrible accident," Zerif said. "We have already sent an envoy to inform them of the danger they caused and to insist they take their unnatural tests elsewhere."

Abeke nodded. She had hoped General Gar's people hadn't been behind those monsters, but needed to be sure. Their cause sounded just. Everyone deserved to protect their home. Chinwe had called the Greencloaks the protectors of Erdas, but she had always been extremely secretive about the Nectar. And Chinwe was probably one of the good ones.

General Gar, Zerif, and Shane all seemed to respect Abeke, and even more, they seemed to need her. They had gone to great lengths to find her and to train her. Perhaps her great stealth would help them get some of the talismans.

Shane took her hand. "It's a lot to take in," he said. "We're involving you in our problems. If you need some time to think this over, just let us know."

Abeke shook her head. Here she stood, with a king asking for her help, along with the man her father had trusted to watch over her, and her first close friend in all the world. There would be time to learn more details later. For now, she would do whatever she could.

Abeke squeezed Shane's hand. "You can count on me," she said. "I'll help you find the talisman."

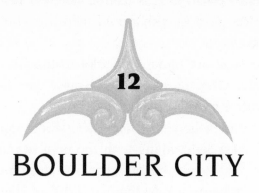

12

BOULDER CITY

FOUR HORSES CANTERED ALONG A FADED TRAIL BORDERED BY low, scrubby bushes. A long, angular ridge occasionally gave variety to the dry, rolling terrain. Rollan rode at the back of the line. A week ago, he had never sat astride a horse. After several days in the saddle, the soreness was wearing off, and he was growing more comfortable with his mount. The horses were all chargers, bred by the Greencloaks not only for power and endurance, but also for intelligence and loyalty. Rollan supposed it paid to have horses furnished by animal experts.

Conor was up ahead, then Meilin beyond him, and finally Tarik in the lead. All wore green cloaks. Olvan had provided Rollan with a gray one.

The commander of the Greencloaks had struck a deal with him. If Rollan helped retrieve this first talisman, he would receive enough money to last him a year, along with the official friendship of the Greencloaks, meaning he could stay in any of the towers and – a point Rollan was careful to include – eat their food. Rollan would receive nothing more until all of the talismans were accounted for, in which case the Greencloaks would buy him a manor and provide him with enough money for five lifetimes. Olvan had stressed that at any point throughout the process, Rollan could renounce his rewards and take up the green cloak instead.

With the crest of a long and gradual rise approaching up ahead, Tarik slowed his mount to a walk, and the others followed his lead. Overhead, Essix gave a cry and came spiraling down to land on Rollan's shoulder. Meilin wore Jhi on her hand, Tarik's otter lay curled at the back of his saddle, and Briggan loped tirelessly alongside Conor.

From the top of the rise, Rollan looked down with the others at a rustic settlement. A few dirt streets crisscrossed the imperfect rows of adobe buildings. People bustled along with a few wagons, horses, and a handful of dogs. Despite the activity, the crowds were nothing compared to what Rollan was used to in Concorba. None of the buildings looked very large to him, and several of them were in shoddy condition. The low wall around the community was made of stacked stones, which Rollan found downright pathetic.

"Our first destination," Tarik announced. "Boulder City."

"'Pebble Village' would ring truer," Rollan scoffed.

"It's also called Sanabajari," Tarik went on. "Nonnatives tend to prefer the nickname. The towns are small here in the far west of Amaya. Few care to brave the dangers beyond the more settled region of the continent. The folk who live here are from sturdy stock. It would be sensible to avoid a mocking tone."

"I see why Amaya is dubbed the New Lands," Meilin said. "No section of Zhong is this . . . uncivilized."

"Zhong is known as the Walled Lands," Tarik said. "The territory within the Wall is highly developed and well-tended. But I have seen corners of the continent beyond the Wall that make Boulder City appear refined."

"This is where we'll find the bear and the raccoon?" Conor asked.

"If Lenori and Olvan interpreted the vision properly," Tarik said. "Barlow and Monte used to be Greencloaks at Sunset Tower. They broke their oaths to become explorers. They've spent the last fifteen years roaming the wilds of western Amaya. Few, if any, have traveled this continent as widely. I've not met them personally, but by reputation they're expert outdoorsmen. Barlow's companion is a bear, and Monte's is a raccoon. Perhaps they've come across Arax in their wanderings. That's the hope, at any rate."

"How do we know they'll be here?" Rollan asked.

"We don't," Tarik admitted. "Greencloaks try to stay aware of their own, present and former. Last we had word, Barlow and Monte had established a trading post in Boulder City. If they're not here, we'll pick up a trail."

They rode down a slope, through a gap in the low stone wall, and onward into town. Rollan noticed the cold stares from people on the street and in doorways, most eyes dwelling on the green cloaks worn by the other members of the group. Nearly all of the people in view were men. The majority were hardy and weathered, with threadbare clothes and rough beards.

Tarik pulled up in front of the largest building in town, a dingy white two-story structure with an amber tiled roof. A covered wooden boardwalk wrapped around the establishment, and a sizable sign proclaimed it the trading post.

In a flash, Tarik's otter became a design on his arm. "Send your falcon aloft," the Greencloak suggested to Rollan. "Conor, leave Briggan outside."

"Essix, take to the—" Rollan began, but his falcon sprang into flight before he could finish.

"Would you mind guarding the horses, Briggan?" Conor asked.

The wolf sniffed Conor's mount, then sat nearby.

"Will there be trouble?" Rollan wondered. He wore a knife at his hip. Living on the streets, he had always carried a small blade of some sort, but the Greencloaks had supplied him with the finest he had ever owned. The weapon on his belt was a true dagger, well-made and keen, almost a short sword. He had a much smaller knife tucked in his boot.

"Perhaps," Tarik said. "Some former Greencloaks hold grudges."

"Interesting," Rollan murmured.

"Should we take off our cloaks?" Conor asked.

"Never out of shame or to win favor," Tarik said. "It sets a bad precedent. We must stand behind who we are and what we represent."

But what do you really represent? Rollan wondered. He watched a group of surly, squinting men go out of their way to walk a wide circle around the Greencloaks. An older man leading a laden mule paused to consider them, one fist on his hip. Across the street, hesitant faces appeared in the windows.

"Everyone is staring," Conor muttered.

"Then let's give them something to watch," Tarik said, leading the way into the trading post. He wore his sword strapped across his back. Meilin had brought her quarterstaff. Rollan noted that Conor left his ax back with his saddle.

Everything screeched to a halt in the trading post as they entered. Diners at the bar paused mid-bite, and trading at the general store came to a dead stop. In the silence, Rollan noticed plentiful animal hides on display, along with outdoor gear and row upon row of axes, swords, and other weapons.

Tarik strode over to the counter in the general store. Several big men made way for him, their gazes ranging from suspicion to outright hostility. Behind the counter a balding man with a mischievous face surveyed the newcomers.

"Greencloaks?" he groaned with a smirk. "Official business or just passing through?"

"I'm here to look in on two former colleagues, Barlow and Monte," Tarik replied.

The man behind the counter looked perplexed for a moment, then gave a nod. "Been some time since those two wore much green. Can't claim to have seen either of them lately."

"That so?" Tarik asked. "Do they still own this trading post?"

"They do," the man replied. "It's the most successful emporium hereabouts, which frees them from minding the day-to-day operations."

Rollan heard a brief uproar behind him. He pivoted

to see Essix gliding toward him through the open door. The falcon landed on his shoulder. Forcing a smile, he stroked the bird with the back of one knuckle, trying to act as though the appearance had been expected. As usual, Essix was out to prove she could go where she wanted, when she wanted, regardless of instructions. Both Tarik and the man behind the counter stared at him. Rollan waved a hand. "Go ahead. Don't mind us."

Tarik turned back to face the shopkeeper. "How long would I need to wait for their return?"

The man folded his hands on the countertop. "They own property all over. They don't share their schedules with me, and it isn't my place to ask. Depending on the season, the two of them can be absent for months at a time."

"He's lying," Rollan blurted, regretting the words as soon as he had let them escape. It was just so obvious. With Essix on his shoulder, his perceptions felt heightened, his alertness sharpened. He could read the way the storekeeper licked his lips at the wrong time, glanced away at the wrong time.

"I agree," Tarik said calmly.

"W-what do you mean, I'm lying?" the man sputtered.

Rollan could feel the men behind him shifting.

"What's the lad playing at?" one particularly large guy muttered to his neighbor. "He's got himself a gyrfalcon."

"Your bosses aren't in any trouble," Tarik said.

The man behind the counter seemed to take some courage from all the grumbling. "Thanks for the assurance, stranger. Look, I'm not sure where you're from, but around here we aren't fond of Greencloaks butting into our affairs."

Some of the surrounding men muttered words of agreement.

". . . no regard for privacy . . ."

". . . holding up the line . . ."

"Go drink your Nectar!"

Tarik stepped away from the counter. He only raised his voice enough to be heard. "I'm here on orders from Sunset Tower. If any man cares to get in my way, step forward."

Rollan noticed that Tarik didn't reach for his sword. He made no threatening movement. But he was a tall man with a serious face, and there was no humor in his tone. The men who had grumbled found other places to look.

Tarik turned halfway back to the counter. "I was trying to be discreet. Apparently that isn't how things are done here. I need to see Monte and Barlow on official business. The orders come straight from the top. You're not doing them any favors by getting in the way. We'll return in force if necessary. They might as well get it over with."

An outburst of murmurs followed the new explanation. The man behind the counter ducked out of sight, as if retrieving something from down low.

Rollan heard faint footfalls. "He's running!"

Tarik leaned forward, looking over the wide counter. Showing unexpected speed, the shopkeeper popped up near the end of it, leaped nimbly over, and yanked open a window.

Rollan ran to chase him. Tarik moved to follow as well, but some of the large customers stepped in his way. With a burst of light, Lumeo appeared, and Tarik started throwing punches.

Essix flew out the window ahead of Rollan, who climbed through in time to see the shopkeeper duck behind the trading post. Rollan hit the ground running. By the time he made it around to the back of the building, the storekeeper was on a barrel, jumping for the bottom railing of a second-story balcony. Before he could pull himself up, Essix swooped at him, talons extended, and raked his arm. The man dropped to the ground.

Rollan kept coming. The man ran toward the far side of the back of the trading post, but stopped short as Briggan raced around from that direction. The shopkeeper raised his hands as the wolf approached. "All right! Chase over. Leave me be."

Conor came around the corner from the same direction as Briggan, just before Rollan caught up to the shopkeeper. "Why'd you run?" Rollan accused.

Briggan moved in close enough to sniff the man, who flinched away. "I've dealt with too many Greencloaks in my day," the man replied. "Listen, I have a thing with wolves. Especially getting eaten by them. Can you call yours off?"

Briggan wasn't growling, but the big animal stood close and had his hackles raised.

"Not so fast," Rollan pressed. "Who are you?"

The man sighed in resignation. "I guess I neglected to introduce myself. Name's Monte."

13

BARLOW AND MONTE

CONOR STAYED AT THE REAR OF THE GROUP AS MONTE LED them through a back room and up a flight of stairs. To think the man behind the counter had been one of the pair they were looking for! He had done a smooth job bluffing Tarik.

Meilin and Tarik had caught up to them behind the store. One of Tarik's eyes had already started to swell, and he had a cut beside his mouth. When asked, Meilin quietly assured Conor that Tarik had dealt out many more injuries than he received.

Under pressure, Monte had promised to bring them to Barlow using a back door. He warned them that his partner might not be happy to see them. Tarik assured him that it was necessary.

As Monte reluctantly led the group down a hall on the second floor of the trading post, Conor noticed a flicker of movement behind him, low to the ground. After they rounded the next corner, he waited, letting the others stroll ahead. A moment later, a furry masked face peered around the corner, ducking back immediately.

"Come on out," Conor offered.

When the raccoon didn't comply, Conor looked around the corner, but didn't spot it anywhere. The little guy was fast.

Conor caught up to the others as Monte knocked on a heavy door toward the rear of the building. It was answered by a brawny man with massive sloping shoulders and thick whiskers that came up nearly to his eyes. He stood almost half a head taller than Tarik, and Conor doubted whether he had ever seen a better human match for a bear.

The huge man glowered at Monte. "Greencloaks! At my door? Really?"

"They . . . uh . . . insisted," Monte explained.

"No surprise there," the big man said, sizing up the visitors. His eyes lingered on Conor. "I see we have some seasoned veterans of . . . what? A week?"

Conor tried to stand up straight and look older than he felt.

Monte gave a nervous chuckle. "They want to have a word with us."

Barlow locked eyes with Tarik. "You looking for trouble? You can't own people. We haven't done anything wrong."

"We're looking for Arax," Tarik said.

Barlow's explosive laugh made Conor jump.

"Arax?" Monte exclaimed. "Is this a prank? Who put you up to this?"

Barlow's barking laugh subsided, but his heavy shoulders kept heaving. He wiped a tear from one eye.

"It's no prank," Tarik said. "The Devourer is back and he's after the talismans. We need to get to Arax first."

Barlow straightened abruptly and he took a shuddering breath. "The Devourer? What kind of talk is this?"

"He's returned," Tarik said. "As promised. Or at least somebody very much like him. Zhong is under attack. The Wall has been breached. Southern Nilo is at war as well."

"This is rich," Monte said. "This deserves an audience. Some lies are too big to swallow, especially on a full stomach."

"I saw the attack on Zhong with my own eyes," Meilin said. "A huge host bearing down on Jano Rion. I left my father behind to defend the city."

Scowling, Barlow turned to her. "Left your father? Let me guess, the Greencloaks took you away."

She nodded.

"When will you people learn to leave kids alone?" Barlow said. "Who first decided to dress them up and equip them like adults? Who keeps the tradition alive?"

"This is a big issue of his," Monte said with a smirk. "Don't engage him. It won't end well. Listen, we're sorry to hear about a war overseas, but we don't know the first thing about where to find a Great Beast, including Arax, so why don't we call this conversation over?"

"You're not bad actors," Rollan said. "The laugh was a little much, Barlow. And you explained too much at the end, Monte."

Barlow considered him soberly. "What's with the gyrfalcon?"

"Take a guess," Rollan said evenly.

With a flash, Meilin's panda appeared, and Essix shrieked from Rollan's shoulder.

"Are we showing off?" Barlow asked, hands closing into fists. "My bear's bigger."

"She's not threatening you," Tarik explained calmly. "Think."

"That's a panda," Monte said, his smirk vanishing. "A silver-eyed panda." He looked at Essix warily, then over at his partner.

"I get the joke," Barlow said gruffly. "It's in poor taste. What is this? Who are you?"

"I left Briggan outside," Conor said, aware that the animals had made an impact on the two explorers. "But he helped me have a vision. I saw a bear and a raccoon leading us to Arax. Olvan and Lenori thought it had to mean you two."

"They've seen the ram," Rollan said. "I can tell."

Barlow was frowning, but looked less hostile. "Let's see the wolf."

"You aren't taking this—" Monte began.

Barlow held up a hand. "Let's see Briggan."

Barlow took his time examining Briggan, Jhi, and Essix after Conor returned. Monte inspected all three as well, but kept his distance from Briggan.

"If this is a ruse," Barlow finally declared, "it's excellent work." The big man ran his hands through Briggan's pelt with reluctant wonder.

"Are you sure you aren't hiding Uraza?" Monte asked Tarik.

"I showed you my mark," Tarik said. "My spirit animal is an otter. We haven't found the girl who called the leopard. Our enemy got to her first."

Conor watched as Monte's raccoon hesitantly approached Briggan, backing away as the wolf sniffed him.

Barlow sat back on his heels. "You want us to believe the big showdown has begun?"

Tarik inclined his head. "The Fallen Beasts have returned, the Devourer is back and on the move – all the things the Greencloaks have worried about for hundreds of years."

Monte shivered. "I'd hoped to be long gone before this day came. Part of me doubted it would ever happen, but it's hard to argue with three of the Four Fallen."

"We need to work swiftly," Tarik said. "We must collect the talismans. Our enemies have the same goal."

Barlow snorted. "This isn't just a race against your enemies. Do you expect Arax to hand over his Granite Ram? He didn't during the last war. Do you think you can take it from him? If so, you don't know him, and you don't know those mountains."

"You do," Rollan said.

"We get it," Monte snapped. "You have a knack. You're onto us. Essix wasn't called Deepseer for nothing."

This was the first time Conor had heard this term. Catching Rollan's eye, he mouthed, "Deepseer?"

Rollan shrugged, his expression perplexed and displeased. Conor could sympathize with the feeling. What other information about their spirit animals were the Greencloaks withholding? Why hadn't they told them all they knew?

"So you've seen Arax?" Tarik asked.

Barlow slowly exhaled. "We've seen most of western Amaya, at one time or another. Splendor like you wouldn't believe. Ugliness too. One day high in the mountains, Scrubber showed us some very peculiar tracks."

"Scrubber?" Conor asked.

"My raccoon," Monte supplied.

"Like the tracks of a bighorn sheep," Barlow said. "But way out of scale. Much too big." He made a shape with his hands nearly the size of a dinner plate. "We followed the tracks some distance. Crazy as it seemed, they looked authentic. We were in high, lonely country. If it was a trick, it was a good one. We knew we might never get a second chance, so we followed the prints."

"He was amazing," Monte said. "Of all the sights we ever saw while crossing unmapped territory, nothing could compare."

"I'll second that," Barlow said.

"Did you engage him?" Tarik asked.

Barlow chuckled. "We were intimidated enough watching from a distance. He knew we were there. He kicked up some wind to remind us who was in charge. When we backed off, he let us go."

"Kicked up wind?" Meilin asked.

"Arax can influence the weather in high places," Monte said. "Especially the wind."

"You really saw a Great Beast?" Conor asked, his face lit with wonder.

Briggan butted his leg.

Conor rubbed his wolf. "I meant a full-sized one."

Briggan butted him again. Conor knew he'd made a

mistake, and hoped he wouldn't have to pay for it later.

Monte glanced at Briggan, then back at the group. "You kids are traveling with legends."

Barlow eyed Tarik. "Those mountaintops are no place for children. They're not even a place for skilled mountaineers. Wait a few years. Let the kids grow up, gain some experience. With the animals they have, they'll be formidable."

Conor couldn't help feeling a little inflated by the praise. He repressed a proud smile.

"It's sound advice," Tarik said. "But we can't. We have to take the risk. It would help our odds to have skilled guides along."

Barlow huffed and scowled. "I respect your mission. But to my mind, the Greencloaks have always been too willing to prey on the young. We get talked into committing to something before we've figured out who we really are. I felt ready at eleven, and I survived, but I've seen other young ones who haven't. The Greencloaks are too quick to sacrifice too much."

"We're in an impossible situation," Tarik said. "We will not find these talismans without the Great Beasts. If the Devourer gets them, that will be the end of Erdas as we know it."

"Aye, but . . ." Barlow sighed. He fixed his attention on Conor, Meilin, and Rollan. "You young ones can't understand. You can't imagine what you're up against. This mission is beyond me and Monte. I expect Tarik has seen and done a lot, but it's beyond him too. We're talking about one of the fifteen Great Beasts. Older than recorded history. Strong enough to level this town on a whim. As comfortable on a precipice as you are in your beds. Smarter and more experienced than we can imagine."

Briggan stepped forward to stand before Barlow, ears pricked forward and head high.

Feeling a surge of confidence, Conor stepped forward as well. "You're forgetting who we have on our side. It's three against one."

Essix stretched out her wings, flapping them twice.

"You've got assets," Barlow admitted. "But they aren't all they once were. You kids need time to grow, and so do they. You'd have to see Arax to grasp it."

"We'll search for Arax with or without you," Tarik said. "Without you I dislike our chances, but we'll still try. Conor saw you in a vision for a reason."

Essix flew to perch on Barlow's shoulder. Jhi rose up on her hind legs with surprising grace. Briggan drew near, bit the leg of Barlow's trousers, and tugged.

Barlow sighed, his posture slumping. He spoke slowly, his eyes on the animals. "I always knew that green cloak would come back to haunt me. I spent years in places no living man has visited before or since, but deep down, in my bones, I knew that sooner or later, that cloak would find me."

Monte glanced at his friend. "Is that how it is?"

"I'm afraid so," Barlow said. "We better dig our gear out of storage."

14

RAVENS

GROWING UP, MEILIN HAD TOURED MUCH OF ZHONG. SHE had visited the Wall in the north, the east, the west, the south, and countless points in between. Thousands of miles long, the Wall enclosed much. But she had never traveled beyond it. She had never explored wild country.

In the weeks journeying with Monte and Barlow, the landscape had steadily become more impressive. What started as prairie grew into hills and high ridges, and finally erupted into mighty mountains. Sharp stone cliffs clawed at the sky, and towering waterfalls fell toward deep gorges. The lower lands were thickly forested, and Meilin caught the sparkle of lakes in the distance, underneath peaks capped in snow. Inside the wall, Zhong's charm consisted mostly of order imposed on the natural terrain. Meilin had witnessed grand feats of architecture – temples, museums, palaces, cities. She had seen elaborate parks and gardens. She knew how water could be channeled to irrigate fields or held in reserve by ingenious dams. She had traveled on wide roads and over glorious bridges.

The splendor here was different. Untamed, unaltered, unmanaged, this beauty surpassed anything she had seen in Zhong. What building could compare to these mountains? What canal could measure up against these unruly rivers and cascades?

Meilin did not voice her wonder. She was not particularly close to any of her companions, and could not help feeling that to praise the magnificence of this wilderness would somehow diminish her and her homeland.

In spite of the remarkable sights, the trek felt long and lonely. Meilin lacked many comforts she had always enjoyed, and missed the familiarity of her family and attendants. Unwilling to get to know her companions through conversation, she relied on observation. Of anyone in the group, she admired Tarik most. He said little beyond what was needful, and had a competent bearing that reminded Meilin of her father's best soldiers.

Monte talked ten times more than necessary. Full of jokes, stories, and idle prattle, he spoke with anyone who would listen. Barlow didn't seem to mind – in fact he made an effort to ride near his friend, chuckling as Monte yammered about nonsense and memories.

Conor spent a lot of time with Briggan. It went beyond talking and petting – he seemed to have no fear of looking ridiculous or of insulting his spirit animal with horseplay. He threw sticks for the wolf to fetch, and ran around playing tag. They even splashed in creeks together. She had to admit that as a result, their relationship seemed to grow warmer. The connection between Rollan and his falcon was much more distant, and Essix stayed aloft much of the time.

Meilin had tried to communicate with Jhi. The day after Jhi rescued her, Meilin had felt very grateful. But their relationship had soon fallen back into the same old rhythms. Jhi was just so docile. The panda liked to play sedately on her own, but showed little interest when Meilin tried to initiate simple games of fetch or catch. Jhi listened whenever Meilin spoke, but offered little reaction. While the group was on the move, Jhi clearly preferred her dormant state, so that was where Meilin kept her.

Only one sleepwalking episode had occurred so far while on the trail with Monte and Barlow. Meilin had woken alone in the dark woods. Jhi had appeared before panic could fully set in, and led her back to the others. The walk had taken more than twenty minutes.

That had happened several days ago. Though Monte claimed they were getting closer to Arax, they still hadn't found any evidence of the ram. This morning they had crossed a wide valley and now they were making their way up a forested slope with little undergrowth. Barlow and Monte rode in the lead. Meilin came behind them, ahead of the boys. Tarik had the rear.

As usual, Monte chattered to Barlow. "Remember that forest on the northern slopes of the Gray Mountains? It was like this one – so much space between the trees, you could practically ride at a gallop. And we found that abandoned outpost."

"Almost abandoned," Barlow clarified.

Monte pointed at him. "Exactly! That one guy was living there all alone. How many pigs did he have? Like a hundred! He was eating bacon for breakfast, pork for lunch, and ham for dinner. And he wouldn't trade one for anything! What a boar, turning his snout up at us so he could hog them all. I wonder if he's still—"

As Essix let out a cry of warning, Barlow reined in his horse and lifted a hand. Monte sat up in his saddle and looked around.

Barlow raised his voice. "We don't want any trouble! We're passing onward to the high country."

In all directions, as far as Meilin could see, men came into view through the trees. One moment nobody was around them, and the next, there were dozens. Armed with spears and bows, they stalked forward together, moving intently, as if approaching dangerous prey. They wore leather about their loins and had capes of black feathers. Some had painted their faces in black and white. A few wore wooden masks.

Meilin's heart pounded, and she squeezed her reins tightly. How had so many warriors managed to encircle them? She tried to stay calm, tried to remind herself that battles were won with the mind. The Amayans had a huge tactical advantage. Meilin guessed there were seventy warriors, with possibly more still out of sight, closing in from all directions. None were mounted, but many had arrows at the ready. Even if Meilin's group tried to ride through them, there was no way to escape unscathed.

Three warriors broke from their pack to address Barlow. The man in the middle touched his fist to his chest. "I am Derawat."

Barlow mimicked the gesture. "Barlow."

"These lands are under the protection of the Ravens. You have no place here."

"We seek no place here," Barlow replied. "We will not remain and will take nothing. We are going to the high country."

"We saw you coming from afar."

Barlow nodded. "We were not hiding. We mean no harm."

"You will surrender to us, so that we may judge you," Derawat said.

In an instant, a huge grizzly bear appeared beside Barlow, a shaggy brute with a hump on his shoulders. The Ravens retreated several paces, weapons clutched warily. The bear reared up to an imposing height, and Meilin felt a pang of jealousy when she considered how Jhi compared.

"We will not surrender," Barlow said sternly. "We are free people going abroad. We have done you no harm. If you insist on trouble, we insist on trial by combat."

The three leaders of the Amayan group conferred. Derawat announced the verdict. "You will choose a champion, as will we. You will compete in our way. If you win, you may pass. If you lose, you are ours."

"Agreed," Barlow said. With a burst of light, his grizzly vanished.

A group of Ravens broke off to form an escort. Tarik rode forward to confer with Barlow.

"How will this work?" Tarik asked.

"If we lose, we belong to them. They can enslave us or kill us as they choose."

Everyone considered that in silence for a moment.

"What is the competition?" Tarik asked.

"Depends on the tribe," Barlow replied, eyeing the Amayan warriors. "Some prefer single combat between humans. Others want spirit animals to fight. Some contests are to the death, others to submission. I've never dealt with the Ravens before."

"Sour luck," Monte grumbled. "Many Amayan tribes are peaceful and fair-minded, even generous. We planned our route to avoid the most dangerous ones and only touched the fringe of Raven lands. They must have spotted us when we crossed the valley."

"Any objection to me handling the fight?" Tarik asked.

"It's best to wait before we choose our champion," Barlow suggested. "They sometimes set strange limits, or use odd weapons. I'm not bad in contests of strength. In a straight brawl between spirit animals, Jools is hard to defeat."

"Very well," Tarik agreed. "We'll wait."

The Amayans led them to a village in a meadow not far off. The dwellings were made of hides supported by wooden frames. Meilin noticed multiple fire pits, but no flames and no smoke. The warriors led the riders to a clearing in the middle of the village.

Derawat indicated a circular patch of dirt. He walked over to a vat just beyond the circle and dipped his knuckles into black sludge. "Two combatants enter the circle. Spirit animals must be dormant. The first to land ten strikes wins. Hard or soft, ten touches ends the contest. I will fight for the Ravens. Name your champion."

Meilin watched with wide eyes as Barlow, Monte, and Tarik leaned together to confer. Should she intervene?

Derawat looked quick and wiry, perfect for the type of competition he had described.

"This is a matter of speed and precision," Barlow said. "Not my strong suit."

"I bet I could do it," Monte said.

"Let me," Tarik said. "Even without Lumeo's help, I have experience with close combat, often with sharp weapons, so I'm used to avoiding blows. I'm quick with a long reach."

"Okay with me," Barlow said.

"I'll face him," Meilin announced.

The three men looked so taken aback that Meilin tried not to feel insulted. They had never seen what she could do.

"He's a large opponent," Tarik began, trying to be polite.

"I wouldn't offer if this contest weren't made for me," Meilin said. "I've been schooled in Zhongese combat arts my whole life. It's my specialty. If any of you attempt this, the outcome is far less certain."

Her companions looked at each other awkwardly. Tarik folded his arms and squinted.

"An answer?" Derawat asked.

"One moment," Barlow replied. Turning back, he said, "Absolutely not. She's too young."

"I'll do it before Meilin!" Rollan broke in. "At least I've been in some scrapes before."

"Meilin," Tarik said gently, "you may be right, but we haven't had the chance to assess your talents."

"I could show you, but I would rather surprise him," Meilin said. "Trust me."

There came a cry from above, and Essix dove down to land on Meilin's shoulder. Meilin tensed. She'd never had contact with the falcon.

"Essix votes for Meilin," Rollan said, his voice stunned.

Meilin watched the falcon soar away, hardly able to believe Essix had endorsed her. How did the falcon know about her skills? She hadn't even realized the bird had been aware of their discussion.

Tarik gave a curt nod. "I won't argue with that. Win our freedom, Meilin."

"You sure the bird wasn't voting against her?" Barlow mumbled.

"I agree with Rollan's interpretation," Tarik stated firmly.

Barlow walked over to Derawat. "Our champion is Meilin." He stepped aside, extending a hand to introduce her.

Meilin came forward, and Derawat recoiled. "Is this your trick to avoid the competition? Only the lowest coward would hide behind a child."

Barlow glanced back at Tarik, who nodded. "She's our champion," Barlow said, his voice betraying his uncertainty. "We're not hiding. Defeat her if you can."

Derawat's eyes blazed. "This is an insult! You claim the least of you can match the best of us! I will not show mercy. You must honor the outcome the same as if I faced a grown opponent!"

"Win or lose, we abide by your rules," Barlow growled. "Ten strikes only. Meilin is our champion."

"There is no honor in this," Derawat spat. "Afterward, you will suffer double for this offense."

Barlow kept silent, but cast a meaningful glance at Meilin.

After Derawat's cape was removed, he stormed over to the vat and dipped his knuckles in the sludge again. Meilin followed him and did likewise. It was neither warm nor cool, and had a thick, greasy feel.

The rest of the Ravens gathered to watch in silence, more than two hundred strong – old and young, male and female. Meilin hoped she was right about her chances. She had no way to gauge the skill of her opponent. What if he had hands like Master Chu? She would lose in two heartbeats.

This was obviously a contest these people practiced frequently. Derawat had the right build and acted confident. His reach would give him an advantage, as would his greater strength. If he connected solidly, she would go down, and he would rain blows on her.

Derawat led Meilin into the circle. He looked down at her fiercely. "Any strike to the arm below the elbow does not count," he said, indicating his forearms. "Anyplace else is a hit. If you step out of the circle, you lose. No second chance. Ten strikes. Mohayli will count."

"I'll be counting too," Barlow put in.

"Questions?" Derawat asked Meilin. "I will still let you choose another champion."

Meilin sized him up. They weren't allowed to use spirit animals in this fight, otherwise she would have let Tarik take her place. The way he could jump and move with Lumeo was unreal. But without help from the beasts, she felt certain that if Derawat could defeat her, he could easily beat any of the others. She had to win. For the mission, for personal honor, for her life.

"No questions," she said.

Derawat's lips tightened and he backed away to crouch into a fighting stance. "Mohayli will start us."

Meilin shook her arms and legs, trying to loosen up. What if the masters she had trained with had all gone easy on her? She knew they often held back, but what if it was more than she realized? What if she was about to be humiliated?

No! Such doubts were poison. She had to keep her head.

A short Raven held up a hand, then dropped it, shouting, "Go!"

"You can do it, Meilin!" Conor called.

She appreciated the sentiment, but would have preferred no distraction.

Derawat danced lightly toward her, lean muscles rippling. She held still, fists ready, stance balanced. He made a couple of fake attacks, but she didn't flinch. Drawing near, he tried to coax her into attacking, but she resisted. First she wanted to determine his quickness.

Growing impatient, he finally took a true swing at her. She dodged it, sliding away from him. He attacked with more vigor, swinging multiple times and forcing her to spin and duck to avoid getting touched.

He was quick. There would be no room for error. She let him back her toward the edge of the circle, positioning herself so that a well-placed punch would push her out.

Derawat took the bait, and Meilin gave him a taste of

her actual abilities. Instead of dodging away, she ducked toward him, slipping under his punch and striking the side and back of his thigh three times, left-right-left, then skipping away before he could retaliate.

"Three," Mohayli called in a surprised tone, holding up three fingers.

Meilin heard Conor and Rollan laughing with delight, but she tried not to savor the small success. She had to stay in the moment.

Derawat looked down at his leg. She had hit him in three distinct places, to ensure the marks from the sludge would be easily distinguished. He gazed at her with new respect, and no longer stepped quite so smoothly. Meilin knew what spots on the thigh would provide maximum discomfort, and she had hit her targets.

Derawat drew near with real caution, his guard up, ready to dart forward or back. It would have been easier if he had remained overconfident.

He attacked suddenly. Twice Meilin felt the breeze from his fist before she blocked the third swing and almost tagged him in the ribs with a counterpunch. He hopped away, hands raised protectively.

His next attacks were more measured, almost hesitant, and he stayed ready to defend himself. Meilin realized she would have to take the offensive. She showed him three subtle feints, and he committed hard to defend the third. Then she slid close and delivered a flurry of sharp blows — stomach, stomach, thigh, side, block, stomach, block, block, knee. She somersaulted away and scrambled to the far side of the circle.

"Five for Meilin," Mohayli said.

"Six," Derawat corrected, wincing. The blow to his knee had been ruthless, and her blocks had hammered the weak parts of his wrists. He was much stronger, but she knew how to focus her blows, and precisely where to land them.

As he tried to walk off his knee injury, Derawat looked at Meilin in disbelief. She returned his gaze gravely. Any gloating would dishonor him and fuel resentment. She ignored the onlookers outside the circle and stayed near the edge as Derawat claimed the center. He shook his head and waved her toward him.

With her hands down, Meilin walked slowly toward him. When he tried a sneaky punch, she avoided it and struck him twice below the ribs.

"Two," Mohayli announced. "That makes eleven for the girl."

As Meilin backed away, Derawat acknowledged her with a nod. She returned it politely.

Tarik, Barlow, Monte, Rollan, and Conor gathered around Meilin, barely restraining their excitement, showering her with astonished praise. The compliments made her glow inside. Only her trainers had ever seen her fighting skills, and they had never praised her like this – like it really mattered.

Tarik placed his large hand on her shoulder. "Meilin, you are full of surprises. I'll be slow to doubt you again, or Essix for that matter. We're lucky to have you."

15

ARAX

ONLY A DAY AFTER LEAVING THE RAVENS BEHIND, SCRUBBER found the first oversized prints. The land around them was completely wild and there was no longer any trail to follow. The three prints were old, preserved when Arax had stepped in a muddy patch that had long since dried.

As the others mounted up to move on, Rollan remained crouched by the prints, tracing them with his finger, trying to imagine the size of Arax. Since the prints were much larger than any the horses made, Rollan knew the ram must be enormous. What ram was the size of a horse? Let alone larger!

"Are you coming?" Conor asked from astride his mount.

Rollan looked up. Having sniffed the prints, Briggan had run up front to travel with Barlow. But Conor had lingered behind.

"Ever herd any sheep this size?" Rollan wondered, rising to cross to his horse.

Conor laughed. "We had some beauties, but none made tracks like this."

Rollan swung up into his saddle. He glanced back at the prints. "Are we sure we want to find this thing?"

Conor shrugged. "If we want the talisman." He kicked his horse into a trot.

Rollan nudged his horse with his heels and matched Conor's pace, staying beside him. "The talisman is supposed to be a Granite Ram, right? At least according to Tarik."

"Yes. Its powers should have something to do with a ram."

"We should just sit back and let Meilin handle it."

Conor laughed. "She was sure something back there."

"I grew up on the streets of a big city," Rollan said. "I've seen – and joined – lots of brawls. Between kids, between adults. But I've never seen anybody fight like her. Not even close."

"Did you see how quick she punched? She could hit me ten times before I hit her twice."

"And she'd block both your tries. Mine too. What are we even doing here?"

"I ask myself that all the time," Conor muttered. "But we have our animals."

Rollan glanced skyward. Essix was nowhere to be seen. "At least you do. What's your secret?"

"I talk to him, I play with him," Conor said. "You see what I do. I'm not giving him secret lessons while you sleep."

"I talk to Essix when she's around," Rollan said. "I feel like she tolerates me. I wish we really understood each other."

"I don't know how much I understand Briggan," Conor said. "We're closer than at first. But he likes to do his own thing too. Run off out of sight. Sniff everything."

"But he comes back. And he pays attention to you."

"Essix comes when it matters," Conor said.

"I guess," Rollan said. "I've always been pretty good at reading people, you know? I had to be, living how I did. Plenty of seedy folks might have hurt me if I wasn't careful. But with Essix helping, even more little details jump out at me."

"That's useful."

"I wish I could get her into the dormant state."

"I have the same problem with Briggan."

Rollan snorted. "The Queen of Perfection has been doing it since we met her. I'd ask how she managed it if she'd ever talk with us."

"We shouldn't be too hard on her. She's probably just shy."

Rollan laughed. "That's one possibility. You don't really think that's all it is, though, do you? I know you're nice, and you were raised in sheep pastures, but you can't be that oblivious."

Conor reddened a little. "Are you saying she thinks she's better than us?"

"I said no such thing . . . but you just did."

"Maybe she *is* better than us."

Rollan laughed again. "You might be right. She sure fights better. She has more control over her spirit animal, she's rich, she's prettier, and her dad is a general."

"We're all on the same team," Conor said. "Whatever

her background, Meilin joined the Greencloaks just like me."

Rollan's face clouded. "I get it. I'm the black sheep. You're all Greencloaks – I'm not. Why are you always pressuring me?"

"That pressure you feel is called a conscience," Conor said, holding Rollan in a steady gaze.

"I wouldn't know about consciences. My mother didn't teach me much before she abandoned me."

"My father rented me as a servant to pay his debts," Conor returned.

Rollan couldn't believe this was becoming a competition. "Look, my terrible childhood is all I've got! Don't you dare try to top it."

That won a reluctant smile from Conor. "You never saw my father in a foul mood," he joked. "But yeah, I guess you win."

"It's nice to win at something," Rollan said.

※

Later that day, the wind picked up. As clouds gathered, the sky darkened to the uneven color of an old bruise. The afternoon grew colder, and Conor showed Rollan how to wrap his blanket over his cloak.

"You need layers," Conor warned as he situated his own blanket around his shoulders. "Once you start to freeze, it's tough to get warm again."

"Think it'll get worse?" Rollan wondered.

"I don't like this sky," Conor said. "I've only seen it like this when harsh weather is coming."

"You've a good feel for it," Barlow said, approaching on his horse. "If we were on flatter ground, I'd worry about tornadoes."

"Tornadoes!" Rollan exclaimed. He studied the ugly clouds. Of course there would be tornadoes. Otherwise fighting the giant ram would feel too easy. "Wouldn't they be worse in the mountains? We'd get blown off a cliff."

The terrain had grown more rugged throughout the day. The ravines were deeper and steeper, the surrounding peaks loomed higher, and the evergreens grew in odd, twisted shapes at this altitude. They passed broad expanses of bare rock and jumbled scree. Rollan didn't like when his horse had to walk near a drop-off, as they were now. He was allergic to the whole falling thing.

"There aren't as many whirlwinds in the mountains as you'll find in open country," Barlow said. "But that doesn't mean things won't get nasty. We could get a windstorm. Rain. Maybe a blizzard."

"We could probably take shelter against that precipice up ahead," Conor said, pointing. "It's angled to provide some overhang, so the rain can't fall straight on us. Unless the wind changes, it should shield us quite a bit. The little pines by the base will give us extra protection. And there's plenty of higher ground in the area to draw off lightning."

"Whoa!" Barlow exclaimed. "Somebody has spent some time outdoors!"

Conor dropped his head, but Rollan could see he was pleased. "I used to herd sheep."

"Monte!" Barlow called. "Conor thinks we should pause at the base of that precipice until we see how the weather is turning."

Monte stopped his horse and scanned the area. "The boy has some sense. I agree."

"Just you wait until we have to scrounge a meal in a bad neighborhood," Rollan told Conor. "Then you'll be glad I came along."

"I'm already glad," Conor said. A big gust almost blew his blanket off. He gripped it tightly until the wind subsided. "You might want to call in Essix."

Rollan looked up. The sky had gotten even murkier, and he couldn't see his falcon anywhere. "Essix!" he yelled. "Come in! There's a storm brewing!"

The wind gusted again, and stinging pellets of grit hit his face. As the wind died down, he heard the clack of pebbles falling around him, but there was nothing above but the open sky.

"Hail!" Barlow bellowed. "Ride for the rock face!"

Something clonked Rollan on the head. It hurt even through his hood. He now saw that what he had taken for pebbles were balls of ice, growing bigger by the second.

Conor broke into a gallop. Rollan dug his heels into his horse and snapped the reins. As his mount started running, the hail began to pelt down in earnest. Hailstones battered the surrounding rocks, ricocheting wildly.

A stone hit him on the hand, shocking him with the force of it. Rollan ducked his head to protect his face. The wind gusted again, full of projectiles. Tarik and Meilin had already reached the modest shelter. Monte would get there next. Then Conor. Barlow was bringing up the rear.

A hailstone struck Rollan square in the forehead. Before he knew what had happened, he had tipped sideways in his saddle and was leaning crazily over the horse's flank. One foot remained in its stirrup, but Rollan's whole weight was off-balance and the ground rushed under him, alarmingly close. Tilting forward, he embraced his horse. To fall on the rocks at this speed would mean serious injuries. His horse slowed to a trot, and a strong hand grabbed Rollan by the shoulder and righted him in his saddle.

"You okay?" Barlow checked, yelling over the wind and the clattering hail.

Considering the circumstances, Rollan figured being alive was the same thing as being okay.

"Let's keep going!" Rollan replied, leaning into the neck of his horse.

The hail was really coming down. The smallest pieces were now as large as Rollan's thumb. Some were almost the size of his fist. He could feel the agitated breathing of the horse beneath him as they raced toward the shelter.

Rollan and Barlow reached the safety of the precipice and swung off their horses. Only when Rollan tasted blood in his mouth did he realize that it was spilling down his face from a gash near his hairline.

Tarik had Rollan sit with his back to the precipice, and the veteran Greencloak produced a clean handkerchief. Hail continued to smash down noisily, but it couldn't hit them directly. Some fragments skipped their way after impact.

Conor helped Barlow and Monte position the horses so they would provide an extra barrier against the wind. Meilin came and crouched beside Rollan, Jhi beside her. The panda leaned over and licked Rollan's forehead.

"Would you look at that," Tarik remarked.

"What?" Rollan asked. Something already felt different.

"Your wound is closing up," Tarik said. He looked up at Meilin. "Did you know what Jhi was doing?"

"I released her and asked her to help him," Meilin said. "Jhi is supposed to be a gifted healer."

"It wasn't a horrible wound," Tarik explained, "but it might have bled a lot. Thanks to the panda, it's clotting already. You're lucky."

"Is that what you call it when an iceberg lands on your head?" Rollan asked.

"It's what I call it when most of the harm is undone," Tarik replied.

Rollan glanced guiltily at Meilin and Jhi. "Thanks. That was kind. I think I can take it from here." He still felt a little woozy, and wasn't sure how much panda spit he wanted on his face.

"Happy to help," Meilin said.

While Barlow and Monte tried to light a fire, Tarik made sure everyone was as bundled as possible. The wind was howling now, but their shelter kept them from the worst of it. The hail shrank to marble-sized pellets, accumulating in drifts.

"I've never seen a hailstorm like this," Monte commented after he gave up on the fire and the group huddled together for warmth. "It can't be coincidence."

"You believe Arax sent it to drive us away?" Meilin asked.

"If so, it'll take more than a little ice," Tarik said.

"Tell that to my skull," Rollan grumbled. "No luck with the fire?"

Monte shook his head.

"Too much wind," Barlow said. "And no good kindling."

Between the legs of the horses, Rollan could see the hail blowing almost sideways now. With growing desperation, he scanned the skies for Essix, but couldn't find any trace of her.

"Do you guys think Essix will be all right?" he asked, almost scared to voice the question.

"She probably found shelter before we did," Barlow said. "Her instincts should keep her safe through worse than this."

"The ice just keeps coming," Monte noted.

"We'll wait it out," Tarik said. "No storm lasts forever."

Rollan nodded vaguely, unsure what they should fear more—the storm, or the ram that had sent it.

The hail finally relented around nightfall. Once the wind died down, Barlow and Monte got a fire going. During the night the chill broke, and by daybreak all traces of ice had melted away.

Not long after sunrise, Essix swooped in looking as sleek and glossy as ever. Rollan welcomed the bird warmly, feeding her from his saddlebags. Despite assurances from Barlow, Rollan had imagined Essix wet and suffering, delicate bones pummeled by hailstones. The falcon acted as though nothing unusual had happened, flying away once she had eaten. Rollan accepted her nonchalance with relief.

After two more days of slow trekking, they found giant ram tracks again. This time Briggan located them before Scrubber.

"Not fresh, but not old," Monte said after examining

some of the sizable prints. "Less than three days. Maybe less than two."

"That's really close," Rollan said. He motioned toward some bushes. "Just to be safe, one of us should stay here and hide."

Monte chuckled. "Maybe two of us."

Rollan worried more than ever as they followed the tracks onward. Part of him had suspected they would never find Arax. It just seemed so far-fetched to actually encounter a Great Beast. But the fresh tracks made the possibility all too real.

They followed a mountain ridge into even more jagged country. The metallic smell of granite dominated the cool, thin air, although they could still detect a hint of pine. Vegetation became increasingly sparse—small, warped evergreens clinging to life in meager patches of soil. At times, their path led along narrow ledges barely wide enough for the horses. As they traversed a section with a dizzying cliff to the left and a sheer rock face to the right, Rollan tried not to think about what would happen if his horse stumbled. It became harder to find prints on the stonier ground, but Briggan never seemed to lose confidence.

In the afternoon, they reached a precarious stretch where the horses could not pass. Everyone collected their essential gear and weapons as Barlow and Monte hobbled the mounts. They proceeded on foot, edging sideways along a narrow lip of rock, backs to the wall. A huge drop yawned just beyond their toes. Rollan envied Essix, gliding on the breeze while everyone else risked a tremendous fall. But nobody lost their balance, and Briggan practically ran across.

On the far side of the ledge, they caught sight of Arax for the first time.

Four peaks were in view, connected by lofty saddles and laced with snow in high, shadowy pockets. The ram stood in the distance, atop a knob of stone, backlit by the sun. Even from afar, they could see he was enormous, the massive head crowned by the curling bulk of his horns. For a moment, everyone stood frozen, and then Arax leaped down out of sight.

"That was a bit closer than last time," Barlow said, stroking his lips with a nervous hand.

"I wish we had more daylight left," Tarik said grimly.

"He saw us," Barlow said. "If we wait to pursue, he could be long gone by morning."

"Then I vote we wait," Monte said dryly.

Tarik, Briggan, and Conor led the way forward. They stepped carefully down and across an incline composed of jumbled stone, like a huge rockslide that had ground to a halt.

Down where the rock-strewn slope ended with a drop-off, they came around an immense stone slab and got a clear view of the widest, longest ledge yet. One side of the ledge bordered the slab – the other fell away to the valley floor. Awaiting them on the ledge was Arax.

The ram stood nearly twice as tall as their largest horse. His coat was dark silver, his thick horns golden. His form was sturdy and strong, with heavy bunches of muscle at the top of the legs and throughout the neck.

Rollan gaped up in amazement. The ram's sheer size made him feel as though he had shrunk. This animal was older than nations, and somehow that long history seemed woven into its majestic presence. This was not a creature you stole things from – it was a creature you revered. Rollan glanced at his companions, who stood awestruck.

Arax's ears twitched. He gave a snort, and his fore-legs stamped restively. Rollan wasn't sure what the ram expected. Were they supposed to speak? Should they run? Bow down? Arax's eyes were unsettling, yellow as raw egg yolks, with horizontally slit pupils.

"You seek me openly," Arax declared in a resonant voice. Rollan wasn't sure whether he heard it with his ears, or just his mind. It seemed impossible that this gigantic beast could speak. "I have encountered two of you humans before. I let you depart in peace. Why have you returned?"

"We were guided here by a vision from Briggan," Barlow said.

Arax cocked his head. "Briggan?" The ram's nostrils flared. "Yes, I see. I sensed uncanny presences. I recognize them now. They are different than when we last met. Briggan and Essix. Their time has come again."

Rollan checked the sky. Essix wheeled nearby, drifting on a breeze.

With a flash, Meilin produced Jhi. The panda sat and stared at Arax.

"Jhi as well," Arax said, tossing his head. "Uraza?"

"Uraza is not with us," Tarik announced. "But she has also come again."

"I welcome their return," Arax said. "They are far from all they once were, barely saplings, but grandeur oft proceeds from lowly origins."

"The Four Fallen have not returned alone," Tarik said. "The Devourer is back."

"Ah," Arax said. "You seek counsel. Old forces have grown active. You can cage a Great Beast, but not forever. Gerathon and Kovo are stirring."

Tarik started. "Is the ape loose? Has the serpent escaped?"

"If not, it will not be long. I am not as sensitive to such matters as some. Tellun is greatest."

Briggan barked.

Arax dipped his horns. "And Briggan, in his time. Some of the others."

"The Devourer will come after your talisman," Tarik said. "With respect, we have come to ask if you would lend it to us. We will need help in the upcoming war."

Arax snorted and stamped, the impact of his great hoof against the rock ringing out like a blow from a sledgehammer. "My talisman? Utter no such folly in my presence."

Landing on Rollan's shoulder, Essix screeched. Her talons bit into him, digging through his cloak.

Rollan swallowed and gathered his voice. "I don't think she agrees," he ventured.

The yolk-colored gaze turned to him. "I understand her much better than you do," Arax rumbled. "The Fallen held that united resistance was the solution. And they fell."

Briggan growled. Essix gave a long cry and stretched her wings. Even Jhi rose up, staring at Arax with uncharacteristic intensity.

"It's also how the Devourer was stopped," Tarik said. "It's how Kovo and Gerathon were caged."

"Should they have been caged?" Arax challenged. "Their hate has fermented. They can't be destroyed, not permanently, not while our order remains. Bad things happen when our kind come together in anger. Better for us to remain apart in our own realms. None claimed my talisman in the previous war, and none will claim it now." The ram once again raised his hoof and struck the rock. "I have spoken."

"Is that it?" Rollan asked in disbelief.

"Please reconsider," Tarik said. "We must have the talisman. Our foes won't relent, so neither can we."

Arax jerked his head high. His nostrils flared twice and his ears shifted. "Traitors!" he bellowed, eyes suddenly crazed. "Many strangers approach! You have lied, for Uraza is with them! You will pay dearly!"

The ram reared up high on his hind legs and heaved forward, charging Tarik.

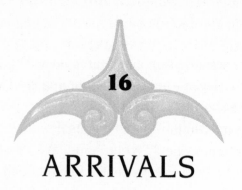

16

ARRIVALS

A S ARAX LUNGED, TARIK DOVE ASIDE, NARROWLY AVOIDING the charge. The ram's huge horns struck the stone slab with the force of an earthquake. Chunks of rock exploded out, and a web of cracks spread across the hard surface. The ledge vibrated beneath Meilin's feet.

Tarik pulled his sword out, and his otter appeared with a flash. Arax sprang again, but this time Tarik flipped gracefully out of the way.

Meilin surveyed the battleground. The ledge was very wide where they currently stood, and ran more or less level before it tapered to nothing in front of them. Beyond the lip of the ledge, a sheer drop awaited.

With a burst of light, Barlow released Jools. The grizzly bear slammed into Arax's rear leg, sliding the ram sideways and forcing him to quickstep to avoid stumbling. Arax kicked out sharply and caught the bear with a glancing blow from his huge hooves that sent Jools tumbling along the ledge.

Meilin raced back to check out the newcomers Arax

had been so angry about. Hopefully Uraza was bringing reinforcements – a second detachment of Greencloaks would come in handy against the giant ram. Meilin curved around the massive slab and peered up the rocky slope.

Ten – no, eleven – people were coming in her direction, from only a short distance away. None wore green cloaks, though several had spirit animals. A Niloan girl ran alongside a leopard, springing lightly among the rocks. The magnificent leopard moved with that peculiar combination of grace and power unique to big cats. The girl was lithe, tall for her age, and advanced confidently. There was a subtle synchronization to their movements, almost as if they were influenced by the same secret music. It had to be Uraza and her partner.

Meilin also saw a baboon, a wolverine, a cougar, a jackal, and an Amayan condor with widespread wings. She had seen all of these creatures in Zhongese menageries, but watching them charge down the slope toward her was a different experience than viewing them in a pen or a cage.

"They aren't Greencloaks!" Meilin called.

"This wasn't an ambush!" Tarik yelled to Arax. "These newcomers have been sent by our enemies!"

The ram charged him again, and Tarik dodged to one side. There was an opening where he could have used his sword, but he didn't take a swing.

"You're all here for the same purpose!" Arax raged. "You want to steal my Granite Ram!"

Rollan, Conor, and Monte dashed over to Meilin while Barlow and Tarik confronted Arax.

"It's Zerif!" Rollan cried.

The man with the sculpted beard raised his head and saluted. A jackal ran near him. "We meet again!" Zerif called, moving closer. "I like the color of your cloak, Rollan."

"Are you here to fight us?" Rollan asked.

"Not if you join us," Zerif replied with a confident laugh. "Sylva, find the talisman."

A vampire bat flashed out from the wrist of one of the women. She clutched it in both hands, eyes closed. A moment later her eyes opened — were they darker? "Done," she said.

"Go get it," Zerif said. "The rest of us will mop up the mess."

The woman headed off while the rest of the group scrambled closer. "Abeke!" Meilin called to the dark-skinned girl. "We've been searching for you. Why are you helping them?"

"She wants Uraza on the right side of the fight this time," said the boy rushing alongside the wolverine. "It's time for the Greencloaks to stop controlling the world."

Hackles raised, Briggan growled. Uraza snarled right back at him. The savage tension between the two beasts made Meilin ready her quarterstaff.

"Back up," Monte advised, retreating behind the sheltering slab. "They're coming down at us. Keep out of sight for as long as possible. Make them fight on level ground."

He was right. Meilin backed up with the others, her stomach fluttering nervously. She had never engaged in actual combat before! Even the fight with the Raven warrior had been a contest with set rules. How would she fare with her life on the line? How dirty might these opponents fight?

Meilin noticed Jhi scraping at a weed that protruded from a crack. "Jhi! Are you going to help me like how Lumeo helps Tarik? We're in trouble. I could use whatever power you can lend me."

The panda gave her a neutral stare, then picked at the weed again. Meilin looked away in disgust.

Conor repeatedly shifted his weight from one foot to the other, ax clutched tightly, his knuckles white. Briggan paced beside him, his fur upright.

"You'll do fine," Meilin told Conor.

He glanced over with a queasy smile. "I've chopped a lot of wood. If they hold really still, I'll do great."

Meilin gave a surprised laugh. It took courage to joke at a time like this.

Rollan stared at the sky. Essix circled high above. "Are you going to help?" he called, obviously frustrated.

Glancing over her shoulder, Meilin saw Barlow on the ground below Arax, trying to avoid the stomp of his massive hooves. Tarik and Jools closed in to assist. When she turned back, an Amayan man sped around the edge of the slab astride a buffalo. She and the others dove out of the way as more enemies dashed into view.

Meilin was only partially aware of the surrounding tumult. Briggan snapping at the underside of the buffalo. Conor holding a mountain goat back with wide sweeps of his ax. Rollan retreating while brandishing his dagger. Monte hurling a stone with a sling. Her primary attention was reserved for the woman approaching boldly beside a cougar.

Meilin crouched into her fighting stance. Jhi raised up on her hind legs beside her. Clutching a spear, the woman sprang toward Meilin, leaping farther than seemed possible, lips peeled back in a hateful grimace. Meilin used her quarterstaff to bat away the spearhead, then spun and cracked the woman on the side of her skull. She crashed to the ground in a boneless sprawl.

Meilin prepared to face the vengeance of the mountain lion. Coiled to pounce, the cougar stared at her panda. The big cat maintained the same pose for several seconds. On her hind legs, Jhi walked toward the mesmerized mountain lion and placed her paws at either side of its head. The cougar's eyes drooped, and it curled on the ground, soundly asleep.

"Better than nothing," Meilin murmured, scanning the area.

Barlow was helping Tarik lead the ram back along the ledge toward the new enemies. Meilin approved of the strategy – let the newcomers help tangle with the biggest threat. Briggan had rejoined Conor. An Amayan man lay on the ground near them, and his mountain goat was retreating from teeth and ax. Monte wrestled with a Zhongese woman whose agile mongoose tussled with Scrubber. He looked overmatched.

Meilin's father had warned that there was little room for sportsmanship on the battlefield. When survival was in question, you fought hard and you seized every advantage, because your enemy was sure to do the same. So Meilin ran to Monte, bashed the woman on the back of her head, and then clubbed the mongoose.

The buffalo charged Arax. Barlow and Tarik sprang clear. Though big and strong, the buffalo looked pathetic compared to the hulking ram. An Amayan man ran behind, shouting for his buffalo to stop. Ram and buffalo came together head to head with a sickening crunch. The buffalo flopped backward, disgustingly crumpled, and the man screamed.

Essix screeched overhead. Looking up, Meilin saw Abeke and Uraza perched atop the stone slab. Harassed by Essix, Abeke tried to aim her bow down at the skirmish. The falcon dove in to disrupt her shot, talons clawing at the girl's hands. Uraza snarled, batting at the bird with lethal paws. Essix shrieked again.

"No, Abeke!" Meilin called. "You're fighting for the wrong side!"

Abeke tried to shoot Essix but narrowly missed. Meilin looked for Jhi, and found the panda carefully climbing the least steep edge of the slab where Abeke perched, down at the far side.

Tarik was locked in sword-to-sword combat with Zerif. Tarik moved like an acrobat, twisting and leaping with vicious grace, but Zerif seemed up to the challenge, deflecting every blow and attacking with astounding speed.

"Meilin, look out!" Monte warned.

Meilin pivoted just in time to dodge a sword thrust from the boy with the wolverine. His saber had a gleaming blade and a gilded hilt. Meilin tried to undercut his legs with her quarterstaff but he jumped the attempt and once again very nearly stabbed her. As she tried to attack with her quarterstaff he chopped it in half, and when she tried to fight with one half in each hand, he quickly shortened both halves with precise strokes. He was skilled and quick, and Meilin doubted whether she could stand against him even if she had a sword.

Backing away, Meilin pulled out her club. It was thicker and shorter than the quarterstaff, and banded with iron.

Rollan came flying out of nowhere with his dagger, but the skillful boy parried the attack and kicked him away. The wolverine got hold of Rollan's arm and shook it viciously.

"You have talent," the boy said to Meilin. "It's a shame you fight against us."

"Your people are invading my homeland," Meilin growled.

"It's a compliment," the boy said. "We admire Zhong. We dream of a better Zhong, free from the oppression of the Greencloaks."

Meilin attacked with her club. He dodged one lightning-fast blow, blocked another, then took the offensive. Meilin backed away, barely holding her own in the onslaught. When he came with an overhanded stroke, she was so busy deflecting it that she never saw the kick that swept her feet out from under her.

Standing over Meilin, saber poised to strike, the boy grinned. "Let me suggest that you yield."

17

GRANITE RAM

FROM HER POSITION ON THE STONE WALL, ABEKE HAD A CLEAR view of the battle. Down below, Zerif dueled a tall Greencloak who moved in ways she had never imagined – twirling and flipping without ever mishandling his sword. Shane fought a Zhongese girl who was putting up surprising resistance considering how young and small she looked. Abeke wanted to help him with her bow, but the pesky falcon kept diving at her, sharp talons threatening her bowstring. Abeke had already wasted two arrows trying to hit the bird at close range.

Uraza gave a low growl. Abeke thought she understood what the leopard wanted. Crouching low, Abeke held her bow near Uraza, nocked an arrow, and aimed downward again. When the falcon flew near, Abeke leaned away and Uraza jumped straight up, catching a wing in her jaws. The falcon struggled for a moment, but after a threatening rumble from Uraza, the bird went limp.

Abeke set the arrow to the string again and bent her bow. It would probably help most if she put an arrow through the Greencloak fighting Zerif. Or she could drop the big guy with the bear. Of course, for now he was distracting Arax, so she should probably leave him alone. The ram had already crushed the buffalo and trampled Neil along with his baboon.

As she searched for a target, the bow trembled in her hand. Did she want to shoot a Greencloak? She had come here committed to help Zerif and Shane get the talisman. But none of this felt right.

The Zhongese girl had a panda. The boy with the ax had a wolf. And the gyrfalcon that had challenged her – was it Essix? She was up against the other members of the Four Fallen. So who was on the wrong side?

Shane and Zerif wanted her to stand with them. Well, truthfully, they wanted Uraza. Abeke frowned. Nobody had shown much interest in her until the leopard showed up. Paralyzed with indecision, Abeke was losing her chance to take action.

The panda approached her unhurriedly from along the top of the high slab, its striking silver eyes set in the black, furry mask. It had to be Jhi, from the stories. Tales told by the fire were coming to life all around her – Greencloaks, Arax the Ram, the Four Fallen. When this new story was told, would she be a hero or a villain?

With the falcon still gripped in her mouth, Uraza watched the panda approach. Jhi looked ridiculous atop the wall, too round and ungainly to cross the thin ridge. Abeke turned her bow toward it.

Uraza looked back at Abeke and growled low in her throat without releasing the falcon. Abeke immediately lowered her weapon. Uraza had never scolded her that blatantly before.

The panda drew near and sniffed Uraza. The leopard released the falcon, which leaped from the slab and took flight. Uraza must have held the bird very gently, because its wing was undamaged. Those powerful jaws could have torn the wing clean off had Uraza desired.

Uraza touched noses with Jhi, then looked up at Abeke and made a purring sound.

"You recognize Jhi?" Abeke asked.

Uraza stared intensely at her with those bright violet eyes. For once, Abeke felt deeply unsure about what the leopard wanted.

Abeke squeezed her bow. If she didn't want to actually hurt any of the Greencloaks, perhaps her safest bet was to run for the talisman. It was why they had come. If she could get it away from here, that might end this bloodshed.

Down below, Shane stood over the Zhongese girl, his blade poised to strike. She was on the ground, defenseless. Then a boy with Shane's wolverine dangling from his arm tackled Shane from behind. Abeke gasped. Blindsided by the attack, Shane went down hard and lost hold of his blade. One of his legs was twisted at an unnatural angle. The girl picked up the sword and held it threateningly. Looking woozy, Shane called off the wolverine.

"We won't fight Jhi," Abeke told Uraza. "But please don't let them hurt Shane."

Uraza turned and sprang from the wall with a mighty roar. It was a fairly long drop, much farther than Abeke would willingly attempt. Uraza pinned the Zhongese girl down with one paw, and the Amayan boy with the other. The girl looked momentarily terrified, but when Uraza fended off a fresh attack from Shane's wolverine with a loud snarl, she glanced up at Abeke. Holding her eyes, Abeke nodded gravely. The girl's expression transformed to one of bewilderment.

Abeke scanned the sky for Essix, and caught sight of the falcon hovering above the main ledge at the point where it tapered down to nothing against the cliff face. Below the falcon, Sylva stood near the edge, watching as her bat fluttered around a small rock shelf well beyond the ledge. She appeared to be stalled. The talisman was probably out of reach, over by the bat. Nobody down below seemed to notice Sylva. Bow in hand, Abeke dashed along the top of the wall. If she joined Sylva, perhaps they could reach the talisman quickly and escape.

Abeke climbed down the least sheer face of the slab she could find, scraping her arms and legs in her haste, and falling the last third of the way. She landed well on the main ledge, and found her leopard waiting.

"We have to get that talisman," Abeke said, running along the ledge at top speed.

Up ahead, the falcon snatched the bat out of the air. Sylva screamed, extending her arms toward her spirit animal. After brutally shaking the bat, the falcon let go and it fell limply, down, down, until it was out of sight. Sylva dropped to her knees and peered over the brink, wailing and calling out for it.

Abeke kept sprinting.

Essix flew to the small shelf beyond the ledge where the bat had fluttered. Abeke could now see that on the little shelf was a rough stone box formed by stacking hefty blocks. The falcon pecked and clawed at it, but couldn't open it.

"Keep away from there!" Arax bellowed, his great voice filling the mountainside with its echoes. "Begone, thieves and deceivers!"

With a sound like a mighty river, a terrible wind blasted along the ledge. It hit Abeke from behind, pushing her forward. Essix was hurled from the shelf and spiraled out of control, striking the wall of the cliff again and again before finding refuge in a sheltered nook.

Abeke remembered Zerif warning that Arax could influence the wind. But a Rain Dancer normally had to labor for days to influence the weather—Abeke had not expected instant gales conjured out of nothing. The violent currents of the wind shifted unpredictably, forcing Abeke to adjust to keep from falling. Uraza ran beside her, fur flattened by the gusts.

Finally Abeke reached Sylva. "How's the bat?" she asked.

"Boku landed on a skinny perch way down there," Sylva replied, looking over the side with panicked grief. "He's hurt."

Abeke considered the shelf with the stone box. It was higher than their present position, and well beyond where the big ledge ended. She noticed some minor ledges and outcroppings in between. She looked at Uraza.

"Think I can make it?"

Uraza nudged her encouragingly.

Abeke's senses grew sharper. She was drawing in Uraza's perception, experiencing her power. As she saw the mountainside in greater relief, more handholds and footholds became evident. Confidence welled up inside. She laid down her bow and settled into a crouch. The wind was blowing at her back. The nearest ledge was well beyond the range a normal person could reach with a jump. But with Uraza's support, Abeke was no normal person.

She ran and jumped, the wind boosting her leap, and skipped off the targeted ledge to a smaller one. She only touched the next ledge once, then stretched forward and clung to a knobby outcropping with both arms, earning stinging scrapes from her wrists to her elbows. The wind howled and swirled around her. Abeke hoisted herself atop the outcropping and sprang again. This time the wind slowed her, and even with the extra power in her leap, she barely caught her next handhold. Abeke steeled herself not to look below. She knew there was nothing but a sheer drop beneath her.

With the deafening wind pushing against her, Abeke pulled herself up. She edged along the thin ledge as far as she could before a final jump brought her to the shelf with the box.

"No!" Arax boomed. "No, no, no, no, no!"

The wind redoubled in force, and the entire mountainside shuddered. Staying low and leaning into the gale, Abeke fought her way to the box. Pushing with all of her might, groaning as she adjusted for maximum leverage, Abeke toppled the weighty lid. Inside she found a granite carving of a ram, attached to a thin iron chain.

The wind abated but the mountainside quaked harder. Some of the nearby ledges and outcrops crumbled away, plummeting down the sheer face into the deep valley below. Praying that the talisman would somehow aid her, Abeke slipped the chain over her head.

Abeke wobbled. The shelf was splitting and cracking underfoot. The whole cliff shook harder than ever. Wearing the Granite Ram made her feel no different, and many of the ledges she had used to get here were gone. But with rocks hailing down from above, and with the rock beneath her tearing away from the cliff, she had no choice but to jump.

She didn't feel the power of the talisman until she sprang, but then it was as though the strength Uraza gave her had been increased fourfold. The leap propelled her farther than she could have hoped. As the shelf tumbled away behind her, she soared an exhilarating distance through the air.

But the jump still wasn't long enough to return to the main ledge, and the other footholds had crumbled. As she began to curve downward, Abeke spotted an indentation in the face of the cliff just large enough that she might find some purchase. Kicking off of the indentation, she gained some height, and with a final push off a meager stone lip, Abeke landed back on the big ledge beside Uraza.

"Incredible," Sylva marveled.

As the wind slackened, the falcon took flight again. Sylva began the dangerous climb down to her bat.

Abeke picked up her bow and turned her attention to Arax. The battle with the ram was moving in her direction. Several people and animals were no longer standing, and Arax fought those that remained with renewed vigor. As Abeke watched, Arax bashed the grizzly bear with his huge horns and sent it sailing off the ledge. The ram barely stopped himself at the brink as the bear plunged out of view.

Then Arax whirled to face her, murderous yellow eyes settling on the talisman around Abeke's neck. With a bellow that shook the mountain, the Great Beast charged straight toward her. Moving fluidly, Abeke sprang to one side, then to the other, but Arax tracked her evasions perfectly. Abeke found her back to the void as the ram closed in, horns lowered to strike.

Roaring with inhuman volume, the bearded man ran forward, wrapped his brawny arms around one of Arax's hind legs, and grabbed hold of it. Skidding to a stop, Arax tried to buck and turn, but the man kept the giant hoof off the ground, his own legs churning forward. Teeth flashing, Briggan attacked another leg. Shrieking, Essix dove at Arax's eyes, talons raking viciously. The huge ram hopped and teetered. With a scream and a huge heave, the bearded man pivoted his body and launched Arax over the side.

The big man fell to his knees as the ram plunged out of sight, following the bear to the valley floor.

Abeke was dumbfounded. Not only had this stranger managed to defeat a Great Beast, he'd just saved her life.

He looked her way, panting. "You . . . you okay, girl?" he asked, holding out a hand to her.

Before Abeke could respond, Zerif lunged forward and stabbed the big man through the back. Abeke screamed, putting a hand to her mouth. The big man pawed weakly at the blade protruding from his chest. The Greencloak with the otter arrived at his side a second later, slashing at Zerif with his sword, but Zerif dodged away, leaving his own sword where it was.

Abeke could hardly believe her eyes. This man, her enemy, had saved her life, only to be rewarded by treachery. A stab in the back. The lowest blow one could deliver. As Abeke drew nearer to her rescuer, Zerif ran to Shane, picking him up. The tall Greencloak got tangled up with an Amayan fighter. The woman's viper struck at him from behind, but the Greencloak's otter bit it just below the head. Though the snake thrashed, the otter refused to let go. A moment later, the tall man clubbed his opponent with the hilt of his sword, knocking her unconscious.

Zerif and the others fled up the rock-strewn slope. He carried Shane over his shoulder, with Shane's saber in his hand. Zerif looked back at Abeke, his eyes frantic. "Hurry! This way!"

Abeke shook her head with a strangely calm certainty. "We're over! I'm not on your side, Zerif!"

At first Zerif looked stunned. Then his eyes became cold and furious. His jackal was with him, uninjured, but Shane's wolverine was limping. Some other survivors had joined them, but they were battered and beaten. All but one lacked their animals. Zerif was out of allies.

Abeke set an arrow to the string of her bow. "Go, or arrows start flying."

After one last withering glare, Zerif turned and started up the mountainside at inhuman speed.

The tall Greencloak turned to Abeke.

"You have the talisman?" he asked.

She took her arrow from the string and fingered the Granite Ram. "Yes."

"And you're with us now?"

"If you want me."

The Greencloak gave a curt nod. "We want you. And we need you. I'm Tarik."

Tarik moved to the side of the fallen bearded man. The Zhongese girl knelt next to him, as did a smaller, balding man with a raccoon. Jhi sniffed the wound where the sword protruded.

"Heal him!" the girl insisted to her panda. "That's what you do, right? Or help me heal him. What should I do?"

"Not all wounds can be healed," the bearded man gasped. "That ram got Jools, but not before my bear gave me one last burst of strength. I've never lifted half so much weight."

Jhi licked the girl, who wept openly. "Save him," she repeated in soft sobs.

The bearded man held the hand of the balding one. "You were the best company a man could ask for, Monte," he said, his voice falling to little more than a whisper. "A real friend." He took a jagged breath. "Don't forget to tell folks I threw a Great Beast off a cliff."

"There will be stories and songs," Monte promised.

"Sorry to leave you early."

"I'll be along by and by," the balding man said, tears falling down his cheeks.

The bearded man looked up at Tarik. As he wheezed, blood dribbled from his lips into his beard. "If it can be managed, dispose of me in a green cloak."

"Nothing would be more fitting," Tarik said.

The bearded man tilted his head back and closed his eyes. Monte leaned close, whispering to him. The bearded man's chest kept hitching in gurgling spasms, then stopped.

"I can't believe he killed a Great Beast," the boy with the wolf said numbly.

"Arax is not dead," Tarik said. "It would take more than a fall, even such a high one. The Great Beasts have too much life in them. Still, if we hurry, we might get away." Though his tone was practical, Abeke thought the man looked very tired. And very sad.

Monte raised his head. "Barlow's gone. I'd rather not leave him here."

"The trick will be getting him to the horses," Tarik said. "We'll manage it."

Uraza snarled in agreement.

"What if they try to ambush us?" the boy with the wolf asked.

Tarik's expression darkened, and he stroked the hilt of his sword. "I honestly hope they do."

THE FALLEN

CONOR LEANED AGAINST THE HIGHEST PARAPET ON SUNSET Tower, looking west, a light breeze ruffling his hair. The tower provided a lofty vantage point, but the mountains where they had confronted Arax were too far away to see. Briggan sat beside him, nuzzling his hand.

They had made it back to Sunset Tower yesterday afternoon. The group had traveled quickly, chased by the constant worry that Arax might catch up with them or that Zerif might stage an ambush. But nobody had troubled them.

Barlow now rested below the surface of a lovely meadow, wrapped in Tarik's cloak. Monte had traveled with them back to Sunset Tower, determined to renew his vows. He hadn't spoken nearly as much on the way back as he had on the way out.

Conor tried not to dwell on certain thoughts. He tried not to picture Barlow or Jools. He tried not to imagine how he would feel if something happened to Briggan. He tried not to guess at all the danger awaiting them, and the other friends he might lose along the way.

Conor stroked the thick fur on the back of Briggan's neck. "I can't believe we're back here. It hasn't been that long, really, but it feels like a lifetime."

The wolf licked his palm. Briggan had only started licking him like that since the battle on the cliff. Conor knelt down and stroked his wolf with both hands.

"Be patient with me," Conor said. "I'll practice with that ax. I stayed alive, and I distracted some of our enemies, but I can do better. Next time you won't have to come rescue me so much."

Briggan nuzzled Conor's forearm.

"That tickles."

The wolf nudged him with his nose.

"What are you doing, boy?"

Briggan stared at him intently.

"Oh," Conor realized. "What do I do?" He had seen the others hold out their arms, so he tried that.

With a flash, Briggan became a tattoo on the back of his forearm. The image burned for a moment, as if his arm had brushed against something scalding. But the searing pain faded quickly.

"I saw that," said a voice from behind him.

Conor turned to find Rollan coming through the door to the top of the tower, his bandaged arm hanging in a sling. Meilin and Abeke were with him, wearing their green cloaks.

"How long have you been doing that?" Rollan asked. "Were you hiding it to spare my feelings? I don't need pity."

"First time," Conor said, showing him the mark. "Really."

"Good job," Meilin said.

"Thanks," Conor replied, feeling shy. Direct conversation with Meilin tended to fluster him. She was just so . . . incredible. And hard to figure out. "I don't think Briggan wanted to become dormant while we were out in the open. My guess is he feels safer here."

"I wonder if Essix will ever feel safe?" Rollan said.

"Give it time," Abeke recommended.

"Where is she?" Conor asked.

Rollan squinted at the sky. "Where she always is — flying around. She likes it when I let her do her own thing. I can respect that."

"She's probably mad because you won't become a Greencloak," Conor said.

"No." Rollan shook his head. "I think she understands. Don't take it the wrong way. I respect you three for joining. I really do. Especially you, Abeke. You've been through so much. But I'm just not sure yet if it's for me, taking official vows and all that. I'm not going anywhere. I'll still help out. And who knows, maybe eventually I'll wear the costume."

"Now that we made it back here, what comes next?" Meilin asked.

"I guess we train," Conor said. "We try to be worthy of our animals. And we find the rest of the talismans. At least, that's my plan."

"Have you dreamed about any new animals lately?" Rollan asked lightly.

Glancing down at his mark, Conor turned away, gazing out at the countryside. "I think we've earned a break."

"You didn't answer the question," Rollan pointed out.

Conor looked down. "Fine. I haven't mentioned this to Olvan yet, or Lenori either, although she gave me a funny look this morning. I don't want to worry anybody, and I don't want to mess up our time to relax, but starting a few days ago . . . I've had these nightmares about a boar."

19

THE RETURN

OCEANS AWAY, ON THE FAR SIDE OF ERDAS, UNDER A BLACK, impenetrable sky, warm rain drenched a large earthen mound on a barren prairie. Blazing strands of lightning zigzagged across the night, offering brilliant glimpses of the cloud ceiling. In rolling bursts, the roar and crackle of thunder drowned out the patter of the raindrops.

The searing flashes of light revealed hundreds of wombats, perhaps thousands, digging along the edge of the muddy mound, like an army of ants working on their nest. Heedless of the tumultuous storm, they burrowed urgently, paws bleeding.

A lone figure strolled among them, watching them dig in the flickering glare of the lightning. They were close. He could sense it.

In one hand he held the crude key, heavy and carved with animal faces. As promised, it had finally been delivered to him. Years of work would culminate tonight.

The hair was standing up on his neck, on his arms. The air hummed. He took several shuffling steps, then crouched low, put down the key, and placed his hands over his ears.

The lightning struck a short stone's throw away, blasting wombats into the air. The thunder was deafening even with his ears covered. He felt the shock through the ground. The muscles in his legs clenched painfully, but the jolt failed to knock him over.

The next electric flash revealed at least a dozen dead. wombats off to his left. The others kept tunneling industriously. It wasn't normal behavior for the animals, but these were not normal wombats. They were in thrall to the presence beneath the mound. He served the same presence, but his devotion was different. At least that's what he told himself.

The figure picked up the key and stood up as the storm raged on. He paced around and around the embankment, the muddy ground sucking at his every step. Eventually, a flash revealed that the wombats had abandoned their duties and massed on one side of the mound.

The figure hastened to that side. As he drew closer, he didn't need lightning to guide him. The key seemed magnetized, drawn toward its destination by an invisible force.

A sharp strobe of lightning revealed the gap in the side of the mound. The wombats hung back reverently. The figure entered the gap and splashed down to his knees as the rain poured down on him.

Holding his breath, the figure plunged the key into the freshly unearthed socket. There came a rumbling, but not of thunder. A tremor rattled from below. He felt it before he heard it, but soon it was as loud as a roar.

The next dazzling blaze of lightning showed the side of the hill tearing asunder. An immense, serpentine form arose, its hood spread, its tongue flicking into the air. Unsure whether he would live or die, the figure bowed down. If his time had come, at least he had accomplished his aim. He had served the presence well.

Gerathon was free.

BOOK TWO:

HUNTED

When the group sets out to find a Great Beast
in Eura, they're betrayed by a familiar face.
Now the team's hunt for the talisman becomes
a race against a powerful enemy.

But the real danger may be
the very thing they're seeking. . . .

You've read the book — now join the adventure at **SpiritAnimals.com**!

Enter the world of Erdas, where YOU are one of the rare few to summon a spirit animal.

Create your character.

Choose your spirit animal.